David's Code

JINGS CHEN

PARTRIDGE
A Penguin Random House Company

To order additional copies of this book, contact
Toll Free 800 101 2657 (Singapore)
Toll Free 1 800 81 7340 (Malaysia)
orders.singapore@partridgepublishing.com

www.partridgepublishing.com/singapore

For my dear late wife Raquel Susana Czertok with love forever

Preface

Around the year 1981 or 1982, it was the fifth year I had spent my life in Buenos Aires and after such a long single life wondering in the City and many places around, far or near and I really settled down my wild horse like lifestyle after I got married with my late wife Raquel Czertok; I arrived Bs. Aires through Montevideo, Uruguay at the very first time at the end of 1977 and looking back to that old time, every guy who is now as my age, younger or older would have different feelings and memories, good or bad, happiness or sadness; but one thing is alwys real, time would never be returned; Buenos Aires for me at that first moment, I fell in love with her at the first sight, it was the same when I met Raquel on February of 1978 and we formed friendship instantly; Well, life used to be looking like as river trip, one never could know what would expect for the next step.....

Raquel used to buy several mgazines weekly and along that period of 1981 and 1982, one popular macazine was called as Sharp or something liked that, it was one of the best seller gossiper magazine in town and you used to find a lot of beautiful and sexy young ladies to show their nice bodies among the pages; it was funny and interesting anyway, I mean the artical they were published along the time, week after week; Once I read an attractive article written something about Hilter's misstress Eva Braun was runing a Kiosko kind grocery shop along Cordoba Avenue between 5300 to 6000 and the magazine also povided a picture with an old lady in his very early seventies; According to Eva Braun was born on February 1912 and up to 1981 and 1982, she was just in her age of 69 to 70; Raquel and me were living on Tucuman 2146 that area was belonging to the area of the huge Jewish town located between Once Plaza and UBA compus and Cordoba Avenue was one of the most fameous avenues in downtown B A City and Eva Bruan's place was only 35 blocks far from our house; I read the news and had a night talk with Raquel, she didn't believe too much about the news but just said that the area from Cordoba 5000 up to Codoba near 6000 and ten blocks extending from both sides of the avenue used to be Nazis residential area that meant that which zone were living a lot of Nazis after 1945; One evening around 5 p.m., I especailly drove our Fiat 125 1978 to visit the place. Yes, I found a grocery, but the girl who was attending the shop told me that la senora went back the south to visit her family; I just bought a box of Marbolo then left the shop; I did so because I was still very young, a kind of passion and curiosity that's all....

After several years, it might be 1985 or after, my business was getting very busy and I had to receive cash or checks personally from some major clients weekly; There was a business friend also a good client whose name was Miquel, well, I don't want to mention his surname and he was a good guy and we were alomst in the same age; every week around Wednesday afternoon or evening I used to drop his shop to collect the weekly payment, sometimes two thousand up to five thousand mixed with cash and checks; whenever I went there not always could catch him, sometimes we set an appointment, he was not in or delaied; so I used to go to a cafe only two blocks from his shop to wait for half an hour or something because I knew he would come for sure.

At that time, I used to wear a very light brown well made fine pilot and carrying a leather made A4 paper sized brief case, it was very popular used at that time in Bs. Aires. The story was that, the cafe I went always was runing byan elder couple and an old guy almost over eighty was working as a waiter; Everytime when I went there, first I parked my car along the side street then first to visit Miquel and after that I used to come back to the cafe to take something fresh or went on to wait for a while; At the begining several times, the old waiter used to come to serve me and after a while; he began to ask me who I was and something; the old waiter's name was also called as Miquel but with German face also carrying strong German accebt in speaking Spanish; well, the old couple never spoke when they were working behind the bar counter and so on, several times after, the owner of the shop began to refuse to charge my bill, I insisted to pay but they didn't want to charge me; anyway I paid the ticket everytime. One day as soon as I arrived the shop, Miquel served me the order and after about ten minutes, he came to sit in front of my table and showing me his passport saying that he was from Yugoslvia, if I couldn't believe in him, I could go to his Embassy which was located at Callao 1100 to check his originaity; I felt so strange and after that, I counted to Raquel the story of the old waiter Miquel; Raquel just said, because that Miquel is a Nazis and he supposed you were one of the Nazis hunters; we laughed. That was just a real story; then in the year 1985, waiter Miquel was about 82 and something; so during the War II, those guys were still in their fopurties or younger, they might be a group of Nazis criminals working in everywhere of their occupied zone.

On February of 1978, a Jewish elder friend presnted mean Argentine Army Colonel whose name was Jose Humberto Sosa Molina who was the son of Lieutenant General Jose Humberto Sosa Molina, the former Minister of War during Juan D. Peron's first Presidency in 1950; the Junior was 57 years old when I met him at the first time and afterwards we were a couple of great friends since his was 30 years older than me; Well, good or bad, I don't want to mention my friend's private life anyway he was my good friend in my life memory always; well, he was not tall but very wide and strong built liked most of the Argentine military guys; he could speak not bad English since he had been studied tank in Dever, Colorado when he was young; we could talk everything between us, once I asked him, how do you think, is that true Adolf Hilter was saved in Argentina and died on his death bed in Patagonia?

Sosa Molina just looked at me and didn't say anything, that meant yes or no, you have to answer it by yourself, but at that time, I felt something special from inside of his eyes, something told me that the question could be yes....

The same, once I met the current Argentine President when he passed by the street very closely, it was in 1979, the next day,

I commented this news to him, he just looked at me with silence but that time I knew what he meant was that don't mention me that piece of shit because Jorge Videla was a criminal who caused the 7 years long Argentina dirty war and more than 30,000 innocent souls vanished away from this world because they were Nazis minded insane killers. Among the missing people during that period, our son Javier Czertok Chen was among them that happened on September of 1983.

It was about the year 1986 or something I couldn't remember, one day my wife Raquel's lawyer friend whose name was or still is I am not sure, Maria Isabel Citerio; she was a very short but kind lady also young at that time; she had a cursin who was runing real estate business in San Temo district, an old and cultural area in southwest of B A City; well, that area was very close to La Boca old port too. Her cursin was called as Marcos, a tall and big Polish guy; Citerio suggested Raquel to buy an old apartment in La Boca, she said that it was a nice flat cheap also big in size; so one Saturday morning, Raquel and me went to visit that flat; it was a not small flat in a big building, on the third or fourth floor I couldn't remember any longer; everything was good both in price and the devision of the interior part but one thing called me attention was that, there was a smalliron made window on the upper part of the same metal made door and every door of the uniformed like apartment around had metal number installing on the door; that meant, each flat of that building was one unit of a big jail house since during the Argentina Dirty War, there were a lot of special jails for different purposes; but that jail house was looking like different; then I told Raquel my discovery and we left the building immediately; the news was that, when we arrived the building gate and ready to go, suddenly we saw a very big factory like plant located just very close to that jail building but by the sea port side and later we had knowledge that, the factory was Argentine government made for waiting Hilter to come and the purpose of that factory was for making Jewish human flesh made soap as they did in Europe; it was something terrible once your eyes touched the scene; I don't know that building is still existing or not, I suppose no.

If I tell you once I saw in a military friend's house, a human skin made lantern lamp cover which was made by human skin, you would say I am a lier but it was a fact, that happened in Buenos Aires also around 80s and of course, the staff was brought from Europe; the owner told me that the skin was cut from the dead Jew's belly part and human skin was perfect for making lamp cover.

There is a fameous antique street in BA city is called Defensa, everybody knows; during the year 80s one could find a lot of Nazis staffs in that area and many antique houses extending in the City; especially Nazis soldier's helmet, SS Uniforms and many many staffs they used in the War II.

There is a town called Qulimes not far from south of Buenos Aires produces fameous Qulimes beer is a town full of German population and where is Universidad de Qulimes located. It is to say, where there is beer where is or was German living joint; other main places like Misiones, Tucuman and most importantly, Patagonia of Argentina; there was a late former Argentine Pesident was from that area, Rio Negro Province; but generally, the whole South America had been the main hidden place of Nazis criminals after 1945; Argentina Chile, Paraguay, Brasil even as far as Bolivia..., and therefore came out Nazis Gold legend...; true or false, one never knows; just like some German deeedented young generations used to say, Holocaust that happened during the War II was a tale or it never did happen.....

Was it a real history or just a piece of South Americn legend? Time will show to the world after couple of decades.

Did Adolf Hilter and his mistress Eva Braun had lived in Patagonia, Argentina? there is no any proof the same as their death that happened at the end of the War? Time will be answered to the history.

Most of main Nazis leader criminals could escape to Argentina after the War; so why Adolf Hilter couldn't do the same while he was the top great chief of Nazis criminals?

Former Argentine military dictator Juan D. Peron was a great Nazis and Facist admirer and he also had dreamed to help Hilter to reform his third Kindom in Argentina that idea affected for a long time Argentine history and also formed Argentine personality.

Raquel and me experienced many decades contact with different levels of Argentine local people and also basing on her local and native knowledge combining her European family history; I had leant quite a lot of real Argentine culture also her history; besides I had been working with Argentine different level of political, social. intellgence and commercial people fro several decades; Argentina had turned to be my second homeland; I knew deeply her flavor of earth also her inner heart.

David's Code is a work of fiction which reflected somehow historical connection up to now, up from the north America down to the deep south of the saying territory; Pam-America used to be a whole body although there are existing some cultural and race difference but they were all belonging to Europe that sourced their originality and you could never devide them into two parts.

Raquel and I experienced even every part of Pam America land along our near three decades lives spending together; I believe her soul would like to see my every works to be present to the world refering her beloved homeland Argentina.

David's Code is ranking one of them.

My memory for her and our missing son together and God would bless us all no matter all we three are living in different world for today and forever.....

August 17th., 2014

Chapter one

Charlottesville, Virginia March 2012

Frank Kennedy put his shopping bag on the kitchen table which just bought from the grocery nearby and went into his studying room thinking to finish the work he planned to prepare for tomorrow's leacher; he is a Vice Professor of History School of Virginia University in his early fourties, a thin and tall guy, somehow a little literature weak looking; he took off his suit jacket first then hanging it on the standing old hanger by the left side of the wide window; the hanger is an antique from his grandpa. The family has been living here since the year 30s, the nice and huge wooden house looking as an antique as well.

After his grandeparents and parents died along the years, his wife Sussy left her a couple of years ago, now he is completely alone; Ana Maria, the Puerto Rican maid come to clean the house twice a week, sometimes he ordered the fast food through phone call from the Kentucky Chicken or the Chinese food joint along the same street he is living, Ivy Street is the name.

Except himself what he could meet by the doorstep used to be the mailmen, fast food dispatchers, plumber or electrican, a couple of neighbors and the cop patrol car that should pass at least a couple of times daily.

Franky opened the room window first, the scene received him is the jade green water of Farmington lake in not very far distance; fresh, clean even flaver like spring wind made him feeling a mere relax also reduced his working stress and loneliness.

He stepped to the desk just next to the window then sat himself on the also an antique armchair thinking to go on working for his subject; he turnned on the desktop, the screen showed a dozon of important emails and most of them were incoming from several major Universities and researching Institutes and many junk mails from nowhere; he deleted first the trash news letters then began to check several major ones at once.

He spent twenties minutes for answering some questions and opinion-exchangings to some long time well-know colleaques acrossing the States; He've got a tough day in the teaching room, a three hours long speech for over eighty specialists, newsmen and private history investigating companies, the question was not the main theme made him exhausted but the complicated post speech O & A. He is a scholar specialized in modern European history and over some side lines covering South American recent topics.

However, Franky didn't followed his Dad's career as a lawyer neither took her Mom's lifetime business as a medical doctor; of course, he never liked his grandfa's career as a military guy; Franky had a step brother who went to South America with his uncle after his Dad's death and Oscar never returned since then.

He got up from the chair and went to the kitchen for fitching a glass of fresh milk and found some French fries leftover of last night also; it was 6:50 p.m., he planned to spend an hour more to build the complete text and then go out for his one-man dinner at Virginia Blue Restauant on the same street.

The desk phone rang. "Yes, speaking..." Franky said lazily. "Hello, Dr. Keanndy, it's Anna, I cleaned your house this afternoon, today is on Tuesday, I couldn't go to your home the day after tomorrow because my aunty is coming from Florida, can I go on Friday instead...?" "Sure, Maria, it's not need to tell me, that's okey, do you wish I pay you something also, you might spend some bucks for your aunt?"

It's okey, Professor, I just want to ask an excuse." Maria said. "Then, have a good time." Franky cut the line off.

He sipped a mouthful milk and intending to make a couple of minutes break, the phone rang again.

"Maria, you want anything more...?" Franky said. "Dr. Frank Kennedy?" "Who is speaking please?" the professor got rather suprised. "My name is Dr. Issac Schtok, I am a professor from University of Tel Aviv. I am here in Virginia to visiting you, sorry I call you through this number because the dean of your Faculty gave me your private number." a strong and bright voice saying from the other end of the line. "You mean Dr. Kauffamnn gave you the number?" "Yes, he did." the not so elderly voice said. "Okey, what can I do for you Dr. Kauffmann?" Franky said softly. "Can I go to your house to meet you?" "But it's out of my office time, anything we could talk in my office in the University." "I am now just standing by my car outside your driveway." the man said. "Sorry, sir. Who gave you my house direction, may I know?" "Dr. Kauffmann also gave me your house address too. Professor."

"Is that such an important matter, sir?" "Yes, it's very very important. We need to talk tonight not later." the man said. "If it is so, please just give me a second, I will go to open the door for you." Franky hanged the tube and made urgently another call for Dr. Kauffmann's office, but there was nobody in the office and he urgently dialed his private cellphone too, no response.

Franky got no choice then he decided to answer the door since he considered himself has got no any enemy.

He walked gently to the house door to answer it and at the meantime, the doorbell rang too.

Franky is thin but as tall as six foot, he is still wearing his white shirt and light brown tie.

The person who is waiting on the other side of the house gate is a well dressed middle aged guy around his fourties, he has a wide round face, thick black mustache and beard, semi brown skinned and he stood about five foot ten but very strong built; he is looking like a secret agent than a University scholar.

The sky was not still dark, Franky opened hafe width of the door saying, "Good evening, sir."

The guy in dark blue nice quality suit and the same color tie answered with a gentle smile, "Good evening, professor, it's so nice to meet you."

Franky studied him up to down then opened the full width the door saying. "Nice to meet you too, please come in."

The person named himself Issac Schtok is wearing a white shirt too, his leather made briefcase showed a foreign taste obviously.

Franky led Issac Schtok to the living room then they both sat themselves down.

Chapter two

"Are you occupied or am I bothering you right now, Dr. Kennedy?" the person who named himself Schtok said.

"To tell you the truth, you did, because I am working for my material for tomorrow; Well, but that's doesn't matter, I would like you to tell me briefly." Franky answered like a well educated gentleman.

"Thank you, Professor, but it's a real important matter." Issac put himself just comfortable on the sofa. "Would you like a can of cold beer, that's only I can offer you, you know, I am living alone." Franky said. "Yes, please, I'd love to. You know, I know all about you." Issac said and that made Franky again to feel that he is not looking like a scholar.

Franky went to the kitchen and fitched a couple of canned beers and putting on the matching table. "Help yourself, Dr. Schtok, yes?" Franky said and took one beer for himself. "Very kind, sir." Issac served for himself a canned beer too. "As you just told me, you are from Tel Aviv U.?" "Yes, I am, but I am working for the other part of the Faculty which is actually under our government's project." Franky listend and already got this guy's sense. "So, you are not really a scientist, aren't you?" "Not exactly, Dr. Kennedy; I used to be, but right now

I am working under our government's order, you know." Issac drank a mouthful cold beer.

"So, what you really want from me?" "Oh, I had already talked with Dr. Kauffmann as soon as I arrived to Virginia and he agreed to allow you to cooperate with me for the project." "Sorry, what project? I don't understnad." Franky said. "I believe you couldn't know how's the project but I would show you step by step." Issac said. "Dr. Kauffmann didn't tell me anything." "If you don't mind, tomorrow let's meet again at your office and Dr. Kauffmann will also present with another gentleman together and up to then you would know everything we have to do like a historian researching work and I am sure you would like it; But tonight, allow me to tell you something, after you will be finished your text work, please go to your basement to find something of your accient family especially anything of your grandpa because we need that for our project, will you do that." Issac drank more beer from the can.

"Where are you staying? May I know?'" "Sure, Professor, I am living in Gorge Washington Hotel." "And this my name card." Issac picked out a piece of white card from his inside pocket putting on the table." he added. "I only could be free after 3 p.m. in the University, you know." "Don't worry, Dr. Kauffmann set the meeting, not me, he won't confuse the time."

"Then I see you tomorrow, thank you for your time and beer too." Schtok got up and ready to leave. Franky accompanied the stranger visitor up to the house gate.

He went back to his desk with the name card left on the table, it's a normal sized white card written in dark blue ink:

Dr. Issac Schtok
Ph.D in Security Science
University of Tal Aviv
State of Isreal

There is a logo stamped on the central part of the card a six points Jewish lantern stand in the same dark blue color as the national flag of Isreal, some Hebrew letters also printed around the upper side of the logo.

The name card showed Franky something not very pleasant is getting around him.

How did Schtok know that in my basement there are something belonging to my grandpa keeping under?

Chapter three

It was near 10 p.m. after Franky had just finished his paper work but during the time his brain has been traveling around his grandpa's life but that was only caming from his Dady's mouth, he didn't know too much about his grandfather.

He went to the kitchen and found a portion of ready made ham and egg sanwitch also served himself half a glass of red wine; He set that all on the small round table by the smallkitchen window and through it he could enjoy the night scene of Liberty hill; his thoughts fell into somehow, a kind of endless missing of his deceased wife Sussy, it has already been two years and a half, his grief and lasting sorrow are getting day by day worse along the time; he is now 42, Sussy was a couple of years older than him and she was too young for die that happened so suddenly and suprisely, it was like a perfect dream they were still dreaming cut by God's will or somehow liked a perfect cake got crashed under Devil's foot, it was wordless heartbroken.

Franky drank the full half glass of wine rushly after he had ate the tasteless sandwich then he got up ready to go down to the basement to see if he could find any clue for the case is happening.

He stepped slowly heading to the staircase which is connecting the ground floor and the basement; it was a short stairway to reach the wooden door of the huge room.

He pushed the door after turning on the light next door and the door easily opened after a gentle pushing. The size of the underground room was almost as big as the first floor since it's a hundred years old house; Maria also did a good job to maintaing it clean and in good order.

It's an open space without any separation, old books, furnitures, different sized cases are all keeping in a prefect condition; in the left rear part of the huge room is keeping several cases of his Grandpa's staffs; those old wooden cases are quite aged; they are all closed but not locked and Franky just ordered Maria to clean the surface dust whenever she went down to clean the whole room. The light is looking a little dim while the evening is getting advanced. Franky found a low wooden stool in order to sit confortably to check the staffs keeping in each big wooden case; he planned to look them one by one.

The first case is containing near one dozon classic flamed paintings and several scrolls, they look like quite valuable but in a very aged condition. Franky took a look for the top one that showing a French style lady with a signature of not famous artist; he rolled up one scroll, it's a Chinese water ink painting signed by the name of Qi Baishi with three different sized Chinese stamps, the scroll is getting faded enough, old light tea color, three black ink painted fishes are swimming on the paper; according Franky's knowledge, the painting at least valued in International auction market for over a couple of million U.S. dollars if it is not a fake one since QiBaishi was considered one of the best Chinese modern artists and along his lifetime, over 40,000 works he had made until his death around 1957; but the painting's age looks like over 100 years that might be a work made by Qi baishi when he was 20, it was the year 1914, it could not be since Qi Baishi was a young capenter then and he didn't start to paint fishes, so if the painting is a real one, its age must be less than one hundred years, more or less 60 or less..., thinking of this, Franky closed back the case lid and let it remaining unlock; it's a better way as he imaged; no literature thief would come in this place without knowledge of such a treasure if those staffs are really big value articles.

Franky went on checking the second big wooden box, what he met as soon as opening the cover, near two dozons Germany written books, very old ones, two sets of German military uniform, old and faded gray color with black cloth made ranks on the collar and shoulders part of the saying coat, a pair of high tube very dark brown color military boots, a military officer hat and some model like staffs.

"Was my grandfa a Germany officer?" that came into Frank's brain; How could it be, my surname is Kannedy, a traditioal Irish immigerant after the World War two. "It must be the same kind of antique staffs that grandpa bought from any flee market." Frank closed the second box.

The third box are containing a lot of old local published book, in different kinds, a jewlary box like small case, a lot of black and white faded photos inside and several old postwar time posters and some broken mechanic driveable toys, cars, planes and military tanks..."

"All of pieces are of waste iron." Franky said to himself. The last case called Franky a lot of attention, bulk of old letters written in Spanish and some in German language, maps, many pieces of map, two handwriting notebooks dated in the year 1965 and besides, several thick paper written different numbers and letters in different order.

Franky stopped to look over other thing since he was getting a little tired; he separated that box out and ready to go back his study room. He got up from the stool and followed the same way back to his studying room; he put the box on the desk first and at the meantime, he found an old lock then returning to the basement gate to lock the wooden door with that small'watching dog'.

The box staying on his desk is a half meter by 30 cntimeter sized wooden case, old fasioned, dark black color, it looks like a an old case older than Franky himself at least. "It might be staffs between the year 1945 up to a965 or something." He thought at the same moment; he cleaned the case surface with alcohol then went to have a warm shower; it was already 11 p.m. when he came back from the bathroom, he locked the case into the down part of his studying room closet then went to bed.

Chapter four

Franky got up next morning and found the time is rather late, he rushly wash up then drove his car heading to the University through the way he usually takes almost everyday, turn to the right to take U.S. highway 29 following up to Barracks then turn right into Everrest Street north right down to the campus of University of Virginia, the place he has been working for near past 15 years. Charlottesville is a quiet and very pleasant garden like town decorated with tons of green trees among wide streets, classic and modern mixed shops, cafes, restrauants along 16th century looking elegant and noble houses; oh, it's a culture coated pretty place; once you have been, you will never forget its beautiness.

Franky rushly got to the Madison Hall of the UV compus, he passed the huge lobby and took the one of the elevators to go to the fouth floor classroom, over two hundred invited guests were already waiting for his arrival; Dr. David Kauffmann, the Dean of the College of Wise neared the microphne to make a short introduction for Dr. Franky Keanndy then inviting Franky to start the leature, it takes about near two hours and following Q &A for 40 minutes more that really let Franky to feel shortage of morning energy.

He stepped back to his office next the door and his private secretary Jacqueline looking his face then make rushly a double coffee to pass to his desk, he drank a mouthful of the hot coffee that just let him feeling a little better; at this moment, Dr. Kauffmann pushed the door in then sat on the chair infront of Franky saying, "Good job, professor." "Thank you sir." Franky is waiting for Kauffmann to say something more.

"Did you meet Dr. Issac Schtok last night?" "Yes, I did, sir." "Good, you know Schtok is now here and I palnned a meeting among we three this afternoon at my office; we have some important things to discuss. meanwhile, I would like you to accompany Schtok to take a view around our beautiful compus and after that to take him to the downtown Chorlottesville to eat something, well on our Faculty's account"

"Sure thing, sir." Franky didn't say no. "Good boy, then see you guys at 3 p.m." Kauffmann got up and ready to leave the room. "Oh, by the way, don't tell Schtok any professional knowledge." Kauffmann stopped by the door side a while saying. "I understand, sir." "Good." Kauffmann left Franky's office.

The office door knoked a couple of minutes later, Jacqueline pushed the door in saying, "Dr. Kennedy, a visitor wants to see you." "Please just let him in."

"Pleae come in, lady." the secretary said to the visitor. Franky said without raising his head. "My name is Rache Perelsztein, Dr.Keanndy." a young lady voice said. Franky rose his head suprisely since he was waiting for Issac Shetok's arriving.

A woman in her middle thirties was standing in front of his desk, she wore dark blue suit, blond hair, very white skinned, she has a pair of very nice and special thin lips coated with very light pink shine, dark blue eyes, she is a very pretty and gentle lady. "Oh, how do you do, lady? what can I do for you?" Franky got up rushly to receive this instant visitor.

"May I sit down?" "Sure, please take a seat." Franky showed the chair by the desk and waiting for the young lady to sit down. "Thank you, sir. allow me to instruduce myself. I am a history researching fellow from University of Warsaw and I am just arriving this town too; I came here not for any offical affair but for a family business." Rachel said while she put her smallleather made briefcase on her knees softly.

"Oh, yes. It sounds interesting, lady." Franky said gently. "Doctor Kennedy, if you don't mind, I would like to talk with you in person and in details; could I go to your place tonight to meet you?" "Sure, I am interseting in the story. I would be free after 8 p.m., this is my card with my home address and phone number too." Franky found a piece of his name card from the desk drawer handling to Rachel over the wooden comfortable antique like wide office desk.

Rachel received it and at the meantime she passes her name card to Franky too.

"Sorry for coming here without advising you, sir." Rachel got up and ready to leave. "That's all right, Miss Perelsztein. Anyway it's so nice to meet you." "The pleasure is mine, sir." "By the way, lady. would you tell me if you know Dr. Issac Schtok?" "No, sir. I don't know who he is?" Rachel said quietly.

"Oh, okey, then I will waiting for you at my house." "Yes, sir, at 8 p.m." "Do you know the streets well of the town, lady?" "No, sir, but I would hire a cab from my hotel." "See you tonight, Dr. Keanndy." Rachel left the office.

Chapter five

About 15 minutes after Rachel's leaving, Dr. Issac Schtok stepping into Franky's office as soon as Jacqueline announced a new visitor's arriving again.

"Oh, Dr. Schtok, nice to see you again, I am just expecting you, please take a seat." Franky said.

"Good day, Dr. Kennedy. I am exppecting your news too." "What news, sir?" "The news about something in your basement." Schtok said smartly. "Last night I was busy in working my text for this morning, you know, Professor Schtok; anyway, sir, I still don't understand what do you really mean?"

"You will find it and you would get a great suprise too." "Okey, since you are mentioning this thing, then I will try to meet any suprise if I could?" "Dr. Kauffmann didn't tell you anything about that?" "What Kauffmann wants is to take you for a sightseeing around our campus. Would you ready do that and afterwards, Dr. Schtok, I would like to invite you for lunch in the downtown; I suppose you would experience the wonderful scene of our town." Franky said. "Oh, sure, I would love to." "Okey, then let's go." Franky accompany Dr. Schtok to get out of the building then began to show him the huge UV's campus around; they took walk together around Rotunda Hall,

Alderman Library, Randall Hall also passing around Tomas Jefferson's stature and others artworks among the campus; Franky introduced him the UV's history since 1819, the year of its fundation and many others historical and culture events; Schtok really received a pleasant lesson.

Franky and Schtok then took ride on Franky's car heading to downtown to visit and eat lunch; shopping malls, theaters, street music shows, Meade Park, City market, Volvo car Store, old clock shop, Chaps ice cream shop. several book stores, especailly red brick made old street houses, old record shops, classic instrument music steet player..., and they end to eat at Henry's Restaurant together with nice and friendly people around the small town.

They drove back to UV's campus at around 2:50 p.m. Kauffmann is expecting for them for a meeting at 3 p.m. in Medison Hall.

When Franky and Schtok stepped into the main office of Dr. Kauffmann, one more gentleman has already been sitting on his right hand chair around the meeting kind of table. "Good afternoon, gentlemen please take a seat." Kauffmann said to the two gents as soon as he met their eyes.

Franky and Schtok chose the two chairs and sitting face to face by the table.

"First allow me to instruce our guest also our future partner Mr. James Smith, the special agent of NSA and he will begin to work with us together as soon as we would plan our scientic project." Kauffmann said. "James, would you please to introduce yourself to our professors and whatabouts our project to be done?"

"Sure, Dr. Kauffmann." Smith said quietly.

"Gentlemen, my name is James Smith, the special agent of U.S. National Security Agency and under an appointed project of our Agency, of course, its also under the permission of our current President to make a research work for a very interesting case; this is why Dr. Kauffmann has also been appointed as the director for executing this project while Dr. Schtok just arrived from Israel to support our plan; we are going to work as a team since now and please be sure that everything is being paid through our Federal account."

The saying guy is a will built, short and nice cut dark brown hair, six foot one coated in a common expensive dark blue suit in his early fourties, especially a pair of dark blue police-like eyes and trained quietness highlighting his personality.

"Would you explain us what is really the project doing?" Franky didn't expect an opening of the meeting likes that. "Good, question; but I would like Dr. Kauffmann first to make a clear explanation for that." James turned his looks on Kauffmann who is sitting and keeping a gentle smile.

"Sure, gentlemen. What we are going to do is simple, research and investigation; well, the first part is to study the case and then for the second part of that, to make a trip and to find out what we need to know, that's all."

"I don't really understand." Franky said. "Well, I suppose, Dr. Schtok is going to tell us the part of this program."

"Dr. Schtok, please..." James eyed Issac Schtok.

"Yes, gentlemen, The State of Israel is interesting in this project then the government of Isreal assigned University of Tal

Aviv to charge the part of investigation, that's why I am here after a long air flight." Dr. Issac Schtok said.

"Am I also a key part of this case?" Franky asked. "You can say that again, Dr. Kennedy." Kauffmann said. "Well, I woul;d like to know the detail since as you say, I am the key person for the project."

"Yes, you do. Dr. Kennedy, you are a cerebrated U.S. history professor especially you are currently working in UV." James said.

"Sure, I am interesting in world modern history, anything to do with that, of course, I would do my best to find out something for the case." "Yes, what you said is only one part of your job, but most importantly, you need to find out your own family history." Kauffmann said.

"My own family history? What's... is that?" Franky almost lost his manner.

"Sure, Dr. Kennedy, you would not understand right now, but it's very important for your homeland as well as mine." Issac Schtok said.

"Well, Dr. Issac Schtok, would you tell professor Kennedy what's the really thing he has to do first?" James Smith said in a mere offical tone.

"Dr. Kennedy, it's the same word that I had told you last night in your house. you have to find something out of your grandpa, yes."

"Very good, gentlemen, today's meeting is just to introducing the main point of our project and from now on, we are all under the official order of Agent James Smith, well, that simplely means, under the rule of Federal Government of the United State of America.

"And this is a very confidential mission, I wish you guys to understand." James Smith said clearly.

It was 4:05 p.m. U.S. Eastern Time.

Chapter six

Franky arrived home after work around 7:00 p.m., he made a shower and changed confortable clothes in order to receive Miss Rachel Perelsztein's visit at 8;00 p.m.

The door bell called at 8 p.m. sharp, he went to answer it; Miss Rachel Perelsztein was waiting by the door step as soon as he opened the front door. "Good evening, Dr. Fennedy." the young lady greeted him with a gentle smile.

"Good evening. lady, welcome to mu house, would you coming in please." "Thank you. sir." Rachel stepped in. Franky led Rachel to go into the big living and inviting the young lady to sit. "Something to drink, lady? Tea or coffee?" "Tea please." the lady said. "Sure." Franky went to the kitchen and several minutes after, he came back with a tray to serve personally a cup of Chinese jasmin tea for Rachel and one more cup for himself. "Please help yourself, it's Chinese jasmin tea, a gift from my college colleaque, a Chinese professor, you know." "Very kind, sir." Rachel said gently. "Yes, Miss Perelsztein, as you had told me yesterday, you are coming from Poland, it's such a long journey, isn't it?" "Yes, I did. to tell you the truth, Dr. Kennedy, I am here with a special mission, half in official and half in my personal interest." "Oh, yes, may I know how is that?" "Sure, sir. officially because our government sent me here to know the detail of your family and personally is that I need to exchange some professional points with you since I am also a modern history investigator working under the program of University of Warsaw." Rachel said while she began to sip the tea. "It sounds so exciting, lady." "Thank you, sir. talking about the official part, what we wnat to know is something about your grandpa." "I don't quite understnad why my late grandpa had got something to do with the government of Poland?" "Yes, it does, Dr. Kennedy.' "I don't really understand since our family was from Irland after the War World II." "Yes, that's only of your personally knowledge, Dr. Kennedy." "What do you really mean?" "What I mean is that your grandfather was not from Irland but from Germany." "How could it be? I have got my birth certificate and everything to show my family history." Franky said. "Sure, you do. but that because your father told you so, the only two persons who knew the secret were your dad and your granddad but I would like to tell you that, it was a pity, they were all passed away." Rachel said. "Okey, Miss Perelzstein, let's just think you are right, but what's secret our family has been hidden that could call your government's attention?" "Good question, Dr.Kennedy, your grandfa's question not only is related with our government but also has something to do with others government." "Oh, that's really suprised me, I didn't realize that my deseased grandfa is still so important that could call a great official attention."

"Yes, he really did, sir." "Miss Rachel, before we are going to speak further, would you tell me if your government has connection with the government of Israel in this case." "I don't think so, sir." "May I know if you know Dr. Issac Schtok?"

"It's an old question, I already told you yesterday, I don't know any Dr. Issac Schtok." "Okey, Miss, your questions also raised my intention to investigate the same case since we are all professional history researchers."

"I am happy to hear that, Dr. Kennedy." "Good, just tell me what can I do for you?" "You need to find out something important from your basement, sir." "Sorry, Miss, how could you know my basement is hidding anything that related with my grandpa's past?" "And, sorry for my question, how could you know the details of the basement of my own house?" Franky added. "It's a good question again, because your own country's intellgence information offered us the details of your own basement, I suppose it makes the things a little clear, sir."

"As you know, anything keeping in my basement is of my own property, is that right?" "100% right, sir. Nobody could violet your own property." "For my own interest, Miss, I would take a better look into the case; but before I will do that, you have to tell me what are you really looking for?"

"I can tell you right now, but one thing I can tell you is that, for you it's a matter of life or death." "Are you threating me?" "Absolutely not, sir. On the contrary, I am trying to help you out." "Why?"

"Because my grandfather was your grandfather's enemy but that doesn't mean you are my enemy; time has been passed but the account still has to be cleared off." Rachel said. "Okey, time is getting later, I have to go back my hotel room in downtown; you have got my name card, haven't you, any news you could call me, the phone number is not from the hotel but of our Polish official unit sited in Virginia." "May I drive you to the downtown?"

"Thank you, sir. I would call a cab." Franky accompaned Rachel up to the door then the lady left into the darkness.

Franky began to feel uneasy after a not short conversation with this Polish young lady; he found the name card she left for him yesterday noon at his office, it was a white fine paper made card written in dark brown letters:

Rachel Perelsztein
Senior Reseacher in Modern European History
Ph.D. in Post War Modern European History
University of Warsaw
Warsaw, Poland

The phone number in Virginia is written in hand writing on the back of the card.

It was 9:15 p.m. Virginia local time.

Chapter seven

Franky was just thinking what Rachel had told him a couple of minutes earlier, the desk phone rang. "Frank Kennedy, speaking please." Franky thought it was a call from Rachel. "Dr. Frank Kennedy? I am a NSA agent, my name is John Stevenson, my co-worker and I are right now by your door, please open the door, please. this is an official matter." a strong and young voice saying.

"Hey, what's that, this is my own property." Franky said. "Yes, you are right, what we need to do is just for your own property, sorry, sir, we are under the order of Mr. James Smith also under the order of the main office of NSA, sir." "Okey, just a minute, I am going to open the door." the instant bothering made Franky feeling quite unpleasant.

Franky lazily walked to the door, first he took a peek through the door eye, what he met were two black suit coated agents standing by the doorstep with a kind of semi-offical looks. "Yes, I am Dr.Frank Kennedy, what can I do for you gents.?" "Good evening, Dr. Kennedy, sorry for bothering so late, we are under an emergency order to confine your house basement, can we come in?" The agent named himself John Stevenson was speaking since his name tag written clearly in black printed letters- John Stevenson."

The both guys are as tall as six foot two or three, John Stevenson already set one step in as soon as Franky opened wider the door. Franky led the two Federal guys into the big living and invited them to sit.

"Yes, Agent Stevenson, now I am here, would you please tell me what's all this about?" "Yes, Dr. Kennedy, it's a very simple case, what we have to do is to confine your basement since right now, that means you are not allowed to go into the saying basement for a period of time, because it's an order under NSA concerning national security matter." Agent Stevenson said.

"Hey, what's hell is that, this is my own house and my own basement." Franky cried. "Please don't worry, it just for a couple of months, here is an offical paper, would you read it and make your innitial, please?" Stevenson handling him an A4 sized document like paper. Franky took a look under his glasses, it's an offical type text and the signature is made by the Director of NSA. "Okey, you guys just do what you want, but I really don't get the sense."

"Well, what we are going to do is just to seal your basement door with our official seal slips and since now no one could cross the door without our permission, it's that simple." "Just do what you want. I would talk with Dr, Kaffmann and James Smith tomorrow morning."

"That's no problem, now please allow us to spend a couple of minutes, you know, we just under the order to fullfill our jobs." Stevenson called his cellphone and two worker-like guy came in and went to the basement door skillfully finished the job. Stevenson got up together with the other agent as soon as the workers did the job.

"Good evening, Dr. Kennedy, sorry for the bothering again." Franky accompanied them up to the door and after they already stepped out in a distance, Franky raised the window curtain to take a look, the two black cars drove off heading to the highway.

Franky prepared a cup of coffee and served for himself, he sat on the living sofa turned off all the lights escept the smalllantern on the maching table beside him. He fell into deep thoughts, what was really happening; it should have something wrong with his deceased grandpa, the reminded Rachel's words.... "If Sussy is still living, then he would have somebody beside him to talk with, at least to exchange some points, but she had gone to the heaven; Franky felt so lonely as a boat wondering on the wild sea.

His mind ran back to his Dady's time then turning back to his grandpa's era; he knows nothing about his grandpa even not too much about his own Dad especial his father died in 1997 at age of 50.

Franky began to make an account of his family tree according his simple memories: Grandpa Hans Kennedy born in 1912 died in 1967 at age of 55. He arrived to America and settled down in Virginia in 1946. Father Jack Kennedy born in 1947 in Viginia died in 1997 at age of 50 when Franky was 25 years old.

This was an very simple account, but why Rachel said his grandpa was not from Irland instead of German? Why NSA came to close his basement tonight with an official order? Why Issac Schtok came at the first night also asked him to take a look in his basement? And this morning during the meeting with Kauffmann, Schtok and James Smith, a special agent from NSA saying they had formed a team to work under a researching project which is actually under national security's concern? And Rachel said she was coming from Warsaw that seems like she is obviously working under the Polish government too. Franky suddenly falling into a deeper thoughts in the semi darkness, he has to do something before something bad will happen......

He remembered that when he was still in teens, one afternoon, he discovered that there was an underground tunner connecting between a small entrance in the rear gorden and the back room of the basement; he need to do something right now, Franky suddenly realized a simple solution.

It was 10:40 p.m. He found a flesh handlight in the closet of the side room then he slipped out of the backward door heading to the entrance he still more or less remembered; it was dark but still under the moonlight; it was not so hard to find the entrance covering by a narrow wooden cap like a door, it was rather dark but under the handlight he found a light switch on the lift side wall of the tunner entrance, he turned it on and illuminated the pathway immediately; he followed the way as he did near three decades ago, the chilhood memories floating up instantly that made him reminding his Dad; he took a deep breath and followed the way up to the other end of the tunner, it took him several minutes to get the small back room of the basement, it was like a secret place and he also found a functioned light that helped him to see everything around that small room; many different sized metal made cases one on the other; he looked over them one after the other and finally he met a special middle sized jewlery box like case that called him much attention; many German language written documents and several old faded pale yellow hard paper with ink drawing, something liked a map and many descriptions in details also with smallmap-like drawings and a couple of black and white faded photos; he decided to take that box back his room after locked back every boxes and doors.

Franky own a house by the east side of River Run lake so he decided to send that box to hide in that old house, at least the house has been long time keeping empty, even nobody knew that house was belonging to Franky, it would be a satety place anyway; thinking of this, he went to his grage immediate and left with that box heading to the place under the moonlight. He took Highway No. 29 heading upwards and connecting No.250 went down passing Wildwood then turned left heading by the right side of River Run lake up to to Franklin and arrived 1260 Stony Point Road where located his old house; it was rather late, nobody around, he went into the house quietly and kept that box in a vary secret place.

He took the same way back when he arrived home it was already 12:15 a.m.

He got relaxed then went to bed after a cold shower.

Chapter eight

The morning next Franky took the routine road heading to the UV to give class for the senior students in Madison Hall. it was 10:30 a.m. after the two hour long leature. he went into his office next to the classroom and just met Dr. Issac Schtok was already waiting for him inside the room.

"Good morning, Dr. Kennedy. sorry for coming in without a privious appointment with you." "That's all right, Dr, Schtok; I am just a teacher, I have got used to meet anybody at any moment; What can I do for you, Professor?" Franky said.

"Yes, Dr, Kennedy, do you still remember the word I had told you the other night at your home?" Issac asked. "Oh, you mean my basement, well, it was just confined by NSA agents last night; so I had got no opportunity to visit it." "Did you go downstairs to check anything?" "No, sir. First of all, I have been so busy and second of all, I really have no idea what is happening with me or, say with my gradfather?" "Look, Dr. Kennedy, as you know, I came so far from my homeland Israel, because it's really an important matter for my country." "But, that's nothing to do with my Grandpa." "Yes, it is." Issac said. "Dr, Schtok, as you also know, my family was coming from Ireland." "Dr. Kennedy, if you don't mind, I would like to tell you a top secret."

"I don't think my family has any secret." Franky said. "Dr, Kennedy, did you realize why the Federal agent James Smith now is assigned to charge the project together with Dr, Kauffmann?"

"I suppose, it's for a national interest in some historical affairs." Franky said. "Dr. Kennedy, if I say there is something to do with your family, you would not offend me, wouldn't you?" "I don't understand. Professor." "Dr, Kennedy, for representating the government of Israel State, I suppose we should have a private talk." "You are gone too far, Dr, Schtok." Franky look at Schtok saying. "Look, for your better benefit and personal security, I suggest you to discuss this matter with me privately." "Then, what you mean is that James Smith is working for the U.S. government?" "Exactly, Dr. Kennedy and he is looking after you because of your Grandpa's affair."

"I don't believe in you, sir. You know, Dr. Kauffmann is my teacher." "You are right, Dr, Kennedy, but Kauffmann is now working for the U.S. government." "What's the problem, I am an American citizen and I am a history professor of University of Virginia." "But, Dr, Kennedy,....., Your grandfather was a traidor." "What did you say? You mean, my Grandfather Hans Kennedy was a traidor?" "We need to talk privatly in a safe place Professor and without Kauffmann and Smith's presence." Schtok said. "Would you call me and come to my place tonight and we should chat at any place but not in my hotel; Well, I would wait for your call after 8 p.m. and you have got my card, yes." "Okey, sir. I will do it." Franky said. "Listen, Dr, Kauffmann will call a meeting at 3 p.m. in this Hall, well, we all have to be presented; My good advice, Doctor, please don't say anythign special but your professional knowledge and I will do the same. Otherwise, the situation will not be good for you. After 8 p.m. we will have a detailed meeting. Now, I have to go. thank you for receiving me, Dr. Kennedy." Schtok got up and ready to leave.

Franky got up also to give the hand to Schtok.

The same afternoon Dr.Kauffmann called Franky to his desk phone saying Agent James Smith is calling a short meeting on the fifth floor to brief some project news, at the conference room 5B; It was 2:50 p.m.

Dr, Kennedy listened just said yes. But his mind was just feeling like a Chinese saying: Deeping in a five miles long fog...."

He took the middle elevator of the three lines birdcages to go up; there was nobody in but as soon as his arriving, every member of the meeting was already sitting on their corresponding chairs. This time, James Smith is sitting on the chairman's place. "Good afternoon, everyone." Franky said and took the last seat to sit himself down.

"Good afternoon, gents. we are here because I need to announce an offical indication concerning our project." James opend the chat box. "Our project is aiming to find something very important that related to the post war history and is still under great concern of the U.S. government as well as the government of Israel State that's why Dr. Schtok is now under our offical progect and as we already know, Dr. Kennedy is the key person for studying also realising our final purpose." James added. "But, excuse me. Agent Smith, would you tell me why I have something to do with this case?"

"Yes, Dr. Kennedy, it's a good question, first of all, you are a celebrated history professor in world mdern history, the second, your grandpa played a very important role in the past; I suppose under these two reasons you can't not out of this project, yes?" "Yes, Mr. Smith, I could catch your sense, but as you know, I suppose, your agency had already confined the basement of my house without any previous notice."

"Yes, we did it because the basement of your house is of U.S. National Security concern and that's why your basement was confined last night. And I would update you one more news is that everything which is depositing in the basement had all been removed this afternoon by our Agency and Dr. Kennedy, this order was personally signed by the President of the United States of America; I am sure my explanition is quite clear." "Oh, I am so pround of hearing that." Franky said ironcally. "Don't worry, everything we are holding will be returned to your hand as soon as the case will be officially considering finished." James said.

"Okey, gentlemen, our brief meeting is finished, anytime, I will let you guys know how to do the next step; as the chirman of this project, I appreciate your cooperation." Kauffmann finally said something. "Do you have something to say, Dr. Schtok?: James asked Issac. "No, thank you." Schtok said with a gentle smile. Okey, Dr, Kennedy, we would like you to present your family history for our next union, would you do that?" Kauffmann said that while he was looking at James Smith. Agent Smith nodded his head.

The short meeting got dismissed, all the guys got up heading to the corridor; James Smith stopped Kauffmann for earing him something. Schtok neared Franky just said in a very low voice, "Tonight 9 p.m. Luis Restaurant, downtown, be my guest." Then he hunried his steps heading to the elevator first and left the building.

Chapter nine

Franky took one more hour class for the fouth grader on the 7th floor of the same building at 4;10 p.m. to 5:00 p.m.; his mind was quite bothering under the afternoon's briefing union, he was still a free bird a couple of days earlier but now he feels that he is a bird in the cage. He intended to finish quietly an hour long leature.

After a cup of coffee in the compus cafe room, he drove back home along the routing path; the traffic used not very rush at any hour that took him around 15 to 20 minutes but this time he paid more attention along the way, it seemed like a black car was presuring him in a far distance especially on the way on No.29, but when he arrived home, he didn't notice any difference. He parked the car into the side grage and went into the living through the connecting door. Franky went directly to check the basement door and he found the door was no more sealed, he slipped himself in and discovered that the room was completely empty with nothing inside. James Smith's word was true, the government had removed everything the same afternoon in the basement on that very afternoon. "You could take off everything, but the most important thing is in my hand." Franky thought.

He went to the bathroom for a shower then took a short nap; it was near 8 p.m. when he woke up and just realized that during that quick sleep he met his late wife came to visit him saying" "You have to be very careful, Franky. beware of everything, everyone and don't get any trouble for yourself since now you are not afford to get any bad thing because I couldn't take care by your side anymore.", Franky knew that it was because he used to miss his late wife very much, therefore he got dreams with her often. He went to the kitchen and made a cup of coffee for himself, while he was thinking the better way to meet Schtok's dinner is to go by a cab and not directly from his house gate. About 8;30 he slipped out of his side door and by purpose to take a short cut crossing the garden to get the end of nextblock of Ivy Road, there were not many passengers around the block; he waved a cab and heading to downtown with the driver and about 15 minutes later the cab stopped only 20 meters far from Luis Restaurant; Franky paid the fare with tip to the elder and silence driver then walking backwards up to the place.

Schtok was waiting for him by the table in the rear side of the not small restaurant; Dr. Issac Schtok wore black suit, pure white shirt without tie; he was looking like a Jewish Rabbi especially with his beard and thick mustache. Franky walked quietly heading Issac's table. "Good evening, Dr. Schtok." "Please sit down, Dr, Kennedy, you know it's so nice we can meet here in such a quiet and safe place." Issac said.

"I suppose you have got something very important to tell me." "Yes, we do have to chat something important; Tell me, did anybody followed your way?" "I don't know, but I tried to avoid it, but why?" "Dr. Kennedy, you should know why? now

49

you are a such an important person." An old waiter neared them to take the order. Franky said something to the elder guy, then the waiter nodded then left the table. "But why? Dr. Kennedy, it's my treat." Issac said. "You are in my town, Dr. Schtok, please be my guest." Issac anwered him a Jewish smile. "Yes, Dr. Schtok, please tell me what do you need from me?"

"Well, Dr. Kennedy, I would like to be straight, could you tell me if you had found anything important from your basement? if you did, pleaase tell me some details; you know, I am from Israel besides, I am working for University of Tal Aviv, in another word, I am working for our government too. What we need right now is to work together. by doing so, you would safe your life and also I could promise you anything you want under the permission of our Gobernment; I suppose you have got my sense, haven't you?"

The waiter came back with a big round tray to serve wine and food by once. "First, I didn't find anything from my basement, the second, NSA had already confined the basement and they also had removed all the things there; So, I have no problem of life or death and I am currently an native born American citizen also a formal professor of UV; do you think I have anything to care about?" "Yes, you do, Dr, Kennedy, because you know one thing but you don't know another thing." Issac said while he began to serve wine for Franky. Red wine with soda, flied chicken with French flies and green salad were of their simple menu. Franky began to eat bread with his chicken, he got really a little hungry. "What I really mean is anything from your granfather." Issac looked at Franky and intending to find some truth from his eyes. "I didn't get any piece of paper.' Franky said.

"Look, Frank, may I call you Frank? you know, Kauffmann is not your friend, James Smith is a secret agent; the only person you could trust is me, I am a history professor too, I am not an agent, my friend." "Kaffmann is my boss, I knew him personally for over ten years. But, Dr. Schtok, I really don't know who you are? you just met me for a couple of days. Am I right?" "100% right, Frank. you know I am coming from such a far way to save you and I am coming here to save my follow people, you know?" "Who is your follow people?" "I am your follow people, Frank.' "Ah, ha.., don't tell me I am a Jew too? Are you crazy?" "Yes, you are, The thing is that you don't really know yourself?" "Sorry, Dr. Schtok, I don't buy your story, it sounds like Jewish bible, it's all written in Hebrew." Franky said. "Okey, I don't want to push you, please take a better look on the paper you have got and think it over and you would find something out, you are a very wise guy, Frank."

They almost finished all the menu along the dinning time. "Sorry, Dr. Schtok, I am feeling a little tired; let's talk for some other time, I would like to go back home right now." Franky waved the waiter ready to pay the bill. "Why don't you come with me to go to my hotel and you could pass the night there. you know, it will be safer." The waiter came again and Franky passed his credit card to him. "What did you say just...?" Franky said. "Yes, I said, you have better to go with me to my hotel and stay there until tomorrow to avoid NSA guys." Schtok said. "Don't tell me they want to kill me?" "I couldn't say no, Dr. Kennedy, if they can't find what they want?" "Just for tonight, Frank, please just listen to me." "Are you an agent too?" "I don't care what are you thinking. just think tonight we are on the same boat, okey." The waiter came back to give him back the card and the receipt.

Franky passed him a twenty bucks note. "Thank you sir, very kind." Franky thought for a short second then said, "Okey, maybe you are right. I go with you and tomorrow morning I could go to the school throught there." "That's my boy." Schtok said.

Schtok and Franky left Luis Restaurant then waved a cab to go to Hotel Milton where Schtok was actually staying, it took ten minutes to reach the doorway of a middle sized hotel. Schtok paid the fare then led Franky to go to his suite locating on the fourth floor. Schtok passed his key-card along the lock-slop and inviting Franky to go in with him. The suite was looking like a small office with a wide bedroom together; Schtok raised the phone tube asking the groundfloor counter to provite an extra single bed also one more set of towel and robe. A dark uniform coated waiter sent the staffs almost immediately. "You know, all my expenses are paying by the government of Israel State." Schtok said. "That's good." "Come on, my friend, first make yourself confortable; do you want to take a shower first?" "Okey, I just want to relax myself a little." Franky said. "Good, now I am going to note something on my desk, please take your time.= After that, I would take a shower too and you know we still have something to talk." Franky made hinself confortable then heading to the bathroom.

At this monent, the door bell rang, Schtok went to answer the room door; what he met were a couple of agent-like guys in their black suit, they both wearing a name tag on their jacket, their mug shots and name also three printed letters written 'HSA'.

"Excuse me, sir, Homeland Security Agency, we are reported that your room now is living a man without registration. May I have your ID please? Since we know you are a tourist from Iarael, aren't you?" one of the agents said. "Yes, I am. I am Professor Issac Schtok of Tal Aviv U. and I am associated with The Embassy of Israel State in D.C." said Schtok. "May I see your ID please, sir?" the agent repeated the same question. "Sure, sir." Schtok went into the romm and found his passport then handled it to the agent. The agent took a peek on the first page of the ID then gave it back to Schtok. "Okey, the same we knew who you are, now please do me a favor to check in your friend's name on the hotel's booking paper. Sorry for bothering your time." The two agents left with a very official manner. Schtok called the front desk saying, "This is Dr. Schtok speaking, please note down my friend's name on your file, Dr. Frank Kennedy, the professor of UV." "Okey, sir, now we are just written on our screen and at the same time it will be turn in onto the HSA's record, thank you!" "Oh, God, In Israel we do it better than here." Schtok said to himself.

Franky just came out of the bathroom in his robe saying, "What was happening, professor?" "Nothing, the front desk called me to see if I need something more."

"Okey, I think I need a short rest and after that let's talk as you said."

"I am going to take a shower berfore sleeping, you may go to bed directly." "You don't want to talk for something important more?" "Yes, I did. But not now, you know our phone is tapped and I suppose your house phone and our cellphones too." Dr. Schtok said.

Chapter ten

Franky arrived his UV office next morning about 9:30 a.m. for giving his class scheduled for ten o'clock. "Professor Kennedy, there was a lady named herself Rachel called at 9:00 this morning, she wish to set an appointment with you." the secretary Kacqueline slipped her head into the door gap saying. "Okey, if she call again just tell her for 12:00 p.m. but in the basement coffderia." "Yes, sir."

Dr. Kennedy met a half dozon post graduated students at the fourth floor classroom to give an advanced topic concerning the interrelation between Isreal and its neighbor countries after 1950; he knew almost everyone for this regular course but at the right up corner of teh room there was sitting a stranger young guy listening silently during the two hours long lesson; Kennedy didn't pay any special attention since it was a common case that happened sometimes.

He headed to the B1 caffideria for feeding himself something likes a lunch; he chose a table and served some food on the TV tray; there were a lot of people at this rush hours for feeding one's stomach; Franky began to take hs soup first then following reading a coupe of printed-out papers he had just received from a foreign institution overseas. "Good day, Professor..." a young female voice appeared by his table, he rose his eyes just met Rachel was standing a foot distance away with her tray in hands. "Oh, Miss Perelsztien. please sit down." Rachel put her tray on the table on which a cup of coffee and a simple sanwitch with cheese and ham. The lady dressed in a set of middle season elegant suit she wore very light pink lipshine; a single piece of ear ring, small but with ancient noble Easteuropean fashion shining and decorated her left ear, it was flashing a piece of smooth and gentle sea water blue with silver shade that attracted Franky's mere attention. "Did you enjoy our small town in these days. Miss?" "Yes, I did. it's really a beautiful town." Rachel began to sip her hot coffee.

"I am glad to hear that, lady." "Did you find something of your grandfather?" Rachel said. "You know, my basement was cleaned off by NSA and I don't know why?" "You mean, everything?" "Yes, everything." Franky said. "I would like to help you but if you are not be honest to me then I couldn't do anything." "What do you mean?" Franky looked at Rachel with a little weird expression.

"Something I know, De. Keneddy."

"I don't think you know anything about my grandfather since I know nothing about him." "Are you now involving in national security matter, is that true?" "They told me that and I am under a job to do investigation over a project." Franky said. "Do you know what kind of project is?" "Dr. Kauffamnn said up to the right moment, I may know the details." "It will be too late up to that moment." Rachel said. "Why did you say that?" "Because I know the details." "Do you mean that you are concerning our national security matter?"

"No, sir, But as you know, I am from Poland and my government gave me a mission to research a very important historical affair, so I have my reason to tell you that." Rachel said quietly. "You know, Miss Perelsztien. According to the project I am involving in just let me feel that everybody knows something but me; I intended to ask them but no one told me the truth; So, how could I believe in your story?" "Yes, Dr. Kennedy, you are right. As such a wise guy likes you, you need to think over the whole case around; I am different than others, I am only working by my government and not for the U.S. part." Rachel said with a soft also low voice. "Maybe you are right, lady; but could you tell me how you could help me out?" "That's very simple, in order you can trust me, let's just make a deal, or for a better saying, your secret to change my secret; do you think it's not fair?" "I have no any secret in hand, if I have any secret that is holding in NSA's hand." "You are not saying the truth, Dr. Kennedy. I know everything you have done during these couple of days; please, just take a look in my eyes..." Rachel said.

Franky rose his head just met the young lady's dark blue and persuading like sights, smooth but powerful. "I just tell you I have nothing to do with my grandfather." "Now the matter is not you have got anything to do with your grandpa or not? the thing is that your homeland has got something very important which is related to your ancient past and the only person who could solve the question is you, the last kin of the matter and which is effect on the U.S. national security also the State of Israel. Now. Dr. Keneddy, do you catch any sense of it?" "Just tell me what is the card in your hand?" "I own the half part of your secret." Rachel said. "What do you mean?"

"You just to take a look on the secret documentary you are hidding, well, there are only a half part of the whole thing, is that clear?" "But, be caution, don't make any mistake before you are going to take a second look on that; because, one false movement, you would cost your life." Rachel added. Franky listened Rachel's words, just stopped drinking his coffee, his mind suddenly opened. "Miss Perelsztien, would you tell me one more thing, are you alone or you are belonging to the group?" Franky said slowly.

"Don't worry about that, I am on my own, you just have to trust me."

"Let me say I am going to trust you, then what's your next step?"

"Up to now, nothing, the first thing you have to do is trying to go on games with your group and don't go anymore to the place where you are hiding your secret; because you are under watching since then; my part of the secret is now under the protection of Polish Embassy in D.C.; it's 200% secured; listen, before the right moment, you can not say any word to anybody; otherwise you will screw up the whole case and you will be lost your life with that." Rachel said quietly. Rachel got up with her finished food on the tray. How can I get in touch with you?" "I will keep in touch with you but not by phone." Rachel left heading to the exit of the Cafederia.

Chapter eleven

A couple of days after, James Smith called a meeting through Kauffmann for a secret place in Flordon, the smalltown located not very far from Franky's house; it was on Saturday morning, when Franky drove to the place was 9:50 a.m. just ten minutes berfore the scheduled time. The rural house is an old enough one, set back about 30 meters from the earth country road. Schtok, Kauffmann and James Smith were already there taking morning coffee around the not big living table, a Virginia country young maid was serving the table, some sweet cookies, samwitches were on the table. Kauffmann and Issac Schtok were talking while Agnt Smith was arranging his paper files. "Good morning, gentlemen." Franky came into the room greeting to everyone. Kauffamnn and Issac greeted back with a smile but James didn't pay attention to Franky keeping work with his pen.

Dr.Kennedy chose the seat just opposit to James and sat himself down. "Gentlemen,..." Agent Smith rose his head saying, "I invite you guys here, because we need more information for the previous part of our project; yes, our agency had studied over the whole material we collected from Dr. Kennedy's basement and we found nothing important for our need; So our

Director suggested me to ask Dr. Kennedy the key information he is still holding in hand. With his secret data we could go on working for the next step. Now we are four members appointed to executing this project and what we need is to work together to fullfill this mission; I would like to say again, this mission is relating our national security; it is under National Security Agency and Homeland Security Agency even FBI's concern and in one word, under the indirect concern of the President of the United States of America; I wish you guys understanding, gentlemen." James said in a serious and very quiet tone." Agent Smith stopped a second then he turned his attention on Franky saying: "Dr. Kennedy, would you tell me what did you find up to now? Time is short." "Nothing, Mr. Smith. I found nothing and to tell you the truth I even don't really understand what do you want? What we are going to do? What is the detail about so celled 'Project'?"

"Let me tell you straight, what we need is something that you still holding in hand, something that is from your grandfather and you know clearly what we want since you are a wise guy. What you are going to do is for our nation not for your grandfather or your father or your family, is that clear?

"Dr. Kennedy...." "But I didn't find anything from my grandfather since your agency had already took off all the staffs of my grandfa." Franky said in a very gentle manner. "Agent Smith, may I ask you what is really looking for? I mean, you just said something of Dr. Kennedy's grandfpa? You have got to tell us clearly, yes?" Dr. Schtok opend his mouth. "It's something very important but very confidential, only Dr. Kennedy can tell you what's that?" "Well, last evening, Mr. Jack

Stevenson, the Asistance Secretary of the White House called me saying, well, there are a couple of old pages written by Dr. Kennedy's grandfather Mr. Hans Kennedy, what we need to find out is those pages innitially." Kauffmann said.

"What do you mean those pages? Dr. Kauffmann? I don't hold any page from my grandfather." Franky said. "Well, the important thing is to find out those pages, well, I believe in Dr. Kennedy, he said the truth, maybe we should find from some others where?" Schtok said with a Jewish smart smile. "Yes, I also agree. I trust Professor Kennedy doesn't have any paper in hand; I know him very well, gentlemen, Frank is my student." Kauffman said while he just finished his breakfast.

"Mr. Smith, I suggest you to check over all the staffs your agency took off from my basement without my permission.' Franky said to James. "As you know, your basement has been confined by National Security Agency of the United States of America, we don't need your permission." James said in his offical tone. "Oh, yes..., I didn't know that, the basement is of my personal property and I didn't do any wrong doing." Franky said. "Yes, maybe you are right, but your grandfather did." James said. "I even don't know my grandfather." "That doesn't matter, Professor." James Smith reduced a little his strong voice; he seemed like begin to believe Franky didn't have any paper in hand.

"Well, gentlemen, the importance is that we have to look it deeper, maybe the pages are holding in someother.s hand." Kauffamnn said.

"Okey, today is on Saturday, how about we stop here, maybe next week we could meet something new..." Schtok said to

James. "Dr. Kennedy, never mind I am pushing you a little hard, you know, I am under an offical duty." James said to Franky. "That's okey, Agent Smith." The country house meeting got dismissed. Kauffmann left first with James Smith and Schtok invited Franky to make a short trip to visit a neighbor town; Franky got the sense and decided to spend the afternoon with Issac Schtok.

Chapter twelve

Franky took Schtok drove on his car heading to Glenorchy, it's a small town not very far from UV compus; They first took Ivy Road through No. 29 crossing Everest street north and turnned down to No. 250 to reach the place.; it was a pleasant and enjoyable midday ride for Schtok as a tourist. "I would like to live in this beautiful and peaceful town, Dr. Kennedy." Schtok said.

"I suppose my car is being wired, well, you could say just beautiful words like that but watch you mouth." Franky said in half a jorky way. "Don't worry, your government would not know if I wish to tell you something important." Issac said. "Tell me Schtok, Israel is something like her?" "Yes, something, but not as peaceful as here, I mean this town." "How is Tel Aviv?" "It's something like New York but full of Jews.' Schtok said kidding. "Are Jews like Americans or we Americans like Jews?" "I would say we jews and you American are very alike in ways of thinking." "But we have a lot stupid Americans here, for example, the asshole likes James." Franky said. "Yes, we have quite a lot sonofbitch Jews there too." "Do you have tons of Agency like here?" "No, we have two Agency but that's enough to shake the world." Issac said. "I know one,

Schtok." "Hey, please don't name it, you car is wired.' "Are you one of them?" "No, Frabnky, I am just a poor professor.' "I don't believe in you, Schtok; you know I never believe in any Jew."

"So, you are an antisemit person." Issac said. "Not really, because you Jews are too smart." "Thank you, but I would ask you a question, do you belive in Nazism?" "No, I only believe in God." Franky said. "Hummm..., that's good, I like you.'" "Come on, Schtok, let me take you to look around the beautiful Glenorchy country; do you remember the country song about West Virginia,... like that, country road...., take me home...., mountain mama, take me home,... West Virginia.... I belong to West Virginia..." Franky said. Colorful mountry, lakes, country road, cowboys, old cottage house with dark red roof, green wall and yellow curtain..., Schtok was enjoying the romantic and beautiful country scene.... "I was born in Virginia, I am an American, Issac, I don't believe in anything but my homeland Virginia..., you know..." "Let's go I am bring you to visit an old farmer who is my friend also was my late Dady's friend, he will buy us a lunch with wine."

Franky drove his antique Blue Bird 1968 traveling along the mountain and streams and lakes, narrow country road colorful rocky and soil and finally reached an old country house not big hidding under green tree bushes, he stopped the engine then led Issac heading to the wooden door of the house, the wooden gate was coated in dark green paint; "Jerry...! Jerry...., opened the door, it's me Franky." Dr, Kennedy knocked the door saying.

"The old man used to sleep up to Saturday noon, you see, he is an old lonely guy." Franky added. "Who is fucking outside, son of bitch..." an elder but strong voice was shouting through inside. After a couple of minutes, a middle sized country man like guy in his early seventies suddenly opend the wooden door saying: "Who is fucking there..., son of bitch, you don't allow me to sleep a little longer..."

"Uncle Jerry, it's me, Franky." Kennedy said. The old guy was about five foot ten, thin but straight, his face looking like an old faded orange, raddish hair with gray beard and mustache, his read and white faded chess square cowboy shirt and a pair of old also faded cowcoy's jeans, but he looked still strong and wild enough. "Oh..., it's you, son, what are you doing here...?" "Uncle Jerry, I bring my friend here to have lunch, I like your smoky carbon made hamberger and red wine.' "No problem, son, what's your friend's name?" "He is called as Issac, he is from Isreal.." Franky said. "Where..? Isreal, is he a Jew?" Jerry said. "Yes, he is, he is a visiting professor in my school." "I just want to kill a Jew, well, you two sons of bitches, just sit by the table outside and I will cook what you want, you just said, smoky hamberger, right?" "Yes, uncle Jerry." "Okey, you two jerks just waiting outside, you like that wooden table and stone stools, well, do what you want and give me a couple of minutes to wash me up then I will cook my shit food for you two." old Jerry wnet back inside. "He is a nice guy but with a dirty mouth.' Franky said to Schtok.

Franky and Schtok sat themselves on the low stone stools around the stone round table by the garden like surroundings.

"Look, Issac, I brought you here, because there is no suitable place to talk saftly because everything is wired after my basement was confined; I really don't know what is going on with my ancient family? To tell you the truth, I feel that you are not on their side and you have got your mission for your country therefore I need to trust you more than my people; Dr. Kauffmann is my former teacher, but he is now working for the government; you should know something that could save my situation; well, the old guy knows nothing, besiders, he cares nothing about the things outside, why don't you show me a piece of way out?" Franky said slowly under warm sunshine and gentle wind.

"I am here to share the project with the UV since my government is concerning the case; you know, Kennedy, because you are the key person who could kick out the first step to find that thing, therefore you are so under care by your dear government. Your government is trying to dig the thing out and our government too; let me tell you straightly, what we want is a piece or several pieces of paper, I am not sure exactly how many, but those papers are the key to find out that important thing, you know and you are a wise guy, you know those paper was holding in your grandfather's hand, now you should understand what I mean, yes?"

"Hey, guys, here you are...." Jerry stepped out from the door with a tray holding with both hands, food and wine are all on.

"Come on, boys, you have wine here, smoky hambergers here, bread, soda; well every thing, look, you guys just enjoy it; I've got to go to find that sexy fucking widow who is living just crossing the river stream for a couple of hours; look, sons, if you want to take a nap just go in to my bed, whenever you want go before my back, just leave everthing here; you got it?" Jerry said. "Yes, uncle Jerry; you just go to enjoy your time.' Franky answered.

Jerry ran away with his old scooter.

Two men just began to feed themselves the food and wine. "Schtok, you've got to give me some idea whar is going to take for the next step because you know the details of the plan, right?" "Well, to be honest and as a foreigner too, the plan is to find something important he did during his lifetime; Kauffmann and Smith knew what's all about, but I really don't know more details, I am an outsider too, they need my help too, you know." Issac said.

"Ummm...., you just have told a piece of the truth, I appreciate that; well, let's say what will be happened if I got no any information in my part?" "They will not believe in you, besides, as you know, they have got enough proof; how do you think, the NSA has nothing to do just want to play with you, you are not so important if they don't concern you, understand?" Issac almost drank all his glass of wine. "Do you like the wine?" Franky asked. "Yes, I do, it tastes something like Jewish wine, very sweety." Issac said. "I would give you a couple of dozons the date you are going back to your hometown." "I will go back to Isreal but would not from here." "What do you mean?" "Because we've got to travel yes or yes, if you will give up your paper to the government or not, it means, you will be out of the question if the case is not completely closed, you know." "Ha...ha..., Dr. Schtok, you finally showed me the truth." "Look, what I shared you here is only between us you know, otherwise we would get good trouble."

"Sure, you won't get worry about that." "But, Dr. Kennedy, just tell me the truth, if you really know something about your grandfather, you better count it to me and maybe I could help you get out of trouble; just take it as a business, if you do it, my government would return your effort...;" Issac narrowed his eyes." "Forget that, what I need is go on my teaching job peacefully in UV." "Too late, Franky. Now you are in and never be out in your lifetime.' "You don't look like a professor, you know." Franky said to Issac. "But, I look like a friend, is that true?"

"I don't think so, you are looking like a Kauffman in Yiddish, yes, a businessman."

"Everything is in business, now Dr. Kennedy, you are in governmental business and there is no way to quit.."

"Say just as you like, well, let's get out of here, I drive you home." Franky said. "Please just drop me off somewhere outside the downtown, I could find my Hotel myself, it's too dangerous to let eyes see we are together." "Okey, I see that, just let's go."

Franky rode back to his house on Ivy Road and left Schtok about two miles away.

He went into the living and found the maid Maria's note saying that she had did the clean job and she would be back on Tuesday morning. It was around 3:35 p.m. and he decided to take a shower then go to bed for a while.

The bell rang at this moment, he went to answer the door directly and meet a young UPS courier agent standing by the doorstep. "Mr. Frank Fennedy?" the young guy said.

"Yes..." "Please sign here." the boy handled him a A4 sized documental like express mail.

Franky received the paper packet just fist granced the title of the sender;

On the left corner of the envelope written:

The Embassy of Poland
in the United State of America
Washington D.C.

The envelop was so light in weight, he opened it and found just an offical letter written:

Jose Neminovsky
The Culture Attache
Embassy of Poland
Washington D.C.

Dear Dr. Franky Kennedy
 On behave of his excellency Mr. Ambassdor Nico Poloaco we have got hornor to invite you to delivery a speech for instroducing the U.S. history during the Civil War.
 Dozons of our local Polish personalities will be presented including our Ambassdor couple and all the members of this Embassy.
 Please be kind to contact me for this matter.

Sincerely,
Jose Neminovsky

It was a thick pale yellow offical paper, Franky read it over and just turned back the page and discovered a hand writting short note:

> Dear Dr. Kennedy,
>
> Just go back right now to UV's libary hall and check a hardcover book on the shelf No. H-22346-1A and you would find a book titled The Modern Europe history by Jimas Park and there is a paper slip attached on page 241, okey I note down the place we have to meet for tomorrow afternoon, it's very important.
>
> Rachel
>
> p.s. please just burn this letter off, because it's the safest way let my message to reach to your hand.

Franky got back to his car rushly heading to UV compus through Ivy Road, he arrived the place 15 minutes later and directly run to the libary hall and got that book, he read the white paper slip on the indicated page written;

> Dito's Cafe 5 p.m.

Franky destroied the paper slip and threw it into the smalltrash box along the libary corridor then left the place.

It was already near 3 p.m. then he quietly to take a long cold shower then went to bed for a nap.

Chapter thirteen

Rachel and Franky met at 5 p.m in Dito's Cafe. and ordered two cups of simple coffee. "Anybody followed you, Dr. Kennedy?" Rachel asked. "What's their concern? They can't not kill me on the street, it's a free country." Franky said. "Yes, of course, it's a free country when you are not involving any political concern." "I never imaged that now I am such an important person after being 12 years a poor professor." "The problem is that you are too rich therefore your government now begin to presue you." "What did you say?" "Nothing." Rachel said.

"Well, why did you invite me to here, Miss Perelsztien?" "Look, it's time I have got to tell you some truth, but you have to seal your mouth forever otherwise one false move, you will be get a great problem, you understand me?" "Okey, please just tell me the news, the thing is getting more interesting day after day." Franky said. "Before I am telling you the truth, you have to be honest to me, because you are still lieing to me." Rachel said in a smooth but cold tone.

"What's a good Polish woman." Franky thought. "Do you hide something in your old house on Stony Point Road?" "What does that mean?" "Please don't go on playing, I know everything. Well, it's good you hide that staff there but now I am telling you something, what you are hidding is only half part of the paper they wanted, the other half part of it is in my hand but not in here the U.S; I will not show it up until the right moment besides with my home government's permission.." Rachel said.

"If you insist to act like that and not using your brain, you will be lost and getting a big problem, do you know that?" "You mean, what I have is only a half of the whole thing?" "Ha.. ha..., you finally got it." "Okey, you just follow my way and you will not be lost." "What's your suggestion?" "Okey, first you have to go to the old house and to remove that box to some other place in the garden, well, sure the NSA agent will track your movement and they will go there to find the paper and they would not get it; so for the next meeting, James Smith will obligate you to give hm the paper, you just promise him but for a couple of days, then I will give you a false one but it will look just like a real one; then they will decide to take a trip to go to many places and you will be the key person to accompany the trip, Kauffmann and Schtok too; Well, I would travel to where you guys are but in undercovered manner; Remember, I am not your friend but your enemy, because our grandfathers were dead enemies to each other; they both only owned one half of that important paper; okey, it's enough for today." Rachel said very seriously.

"Why did you know so detailly?" Franky asked.

"Because it's also under the great concern of Polish Government."

"Are you a secret agent of the Polish Garverment?"

"Not exactly." Rachel smiled.

"Is Schtok an Isreal agent?"

"I don't know, you know, the U.S. and Isreal used to work together."

"Well, Dr. Kennedy, after the next meeting James will be called, you just go to the book store named Tony's in downtown and ask for Joseph and telling him you need to take Rachel's letter then he will give you a sealed envelop containing what you need and you could give that paper to James Smith, then your first problem will be solved immediately.

"You don't need to follow me, I will get in touch with you step by step and please don't worry." Rachel added. Franky listened every word by word

"Good, Dr. Kennedy, I need to go, you just stay here for at least ten more minutes. good luck."

Rachel got up and disappeared after the doorway..

After Rachel's leaving, Franky paid the bill and left the Cafe, he walked a couple of blocks then waved a cab heading to Ivy Road.

It was about 6:10 p.m., he got off from the cab ten meters before his house and went to the grocery at the corner to get something. There were only a copuple of clients inside the small shop.

"Good evening..." Franky stepped into the store just met the owner Mrs. Cunningham was taking care the register. "Hello, professor, how're you doing...?" "I am okey, ma'me and how about you?" Franky answered.

Franky went to the rear side and picked up something he needed, when he returned to the register counter, the other clients had already checked out. Franky put everything on the counter and ready to draw some bills from the wallet to pay the account.

"You know, about half an hour earlier, a black car arrived and two cop like guys went into your house with their keys and after about ten minutes they came out and left away with the car; they both wore dark suit." the elderly lady informed Franky. "Oh, really...?"

"You know, I paid attention for being a good neighbor, you know."

"Thank you, Mrs. Cunningham."

"Be watch your ass, professor.'

"Yes, I sure do, thanks."

Franky left the shop and walking back home, it was just 15 meters in distance.

Chapter fourteen

Franky didn't care what Mrs. Cunningham told him about secret agents visited his house without permission since it was the job they used to carry; the same they couldn't find anything inside the house just forget for it.

He went back home and taking the routine he did every evening; while he was working for the paper for the next day's school text, he was thinking about Rachel's words and he decided to visit the old house to remove the old box to a better place. After a couple of hours of working on screen, it was almost 10 p.m., he took a shower and prepared a small glass of white wine with soda for himself, it was the usuall drink he often took with his late wife Sussy, she has gone for five years already, time flies, her picture with a gentle smile standing by the left corner of Franky's desk; whenever he looked at her, it seemed like Sussy was smiling or talking mentally to him; how good if she was still alive; he would not be so lonely, so sad, so silence in thinking everything, nobody could talk to him in heart; with students, it was just a kind of teaching business; right now, he is involoving in a strange situation; it's nothing to do with his career neither his own business but his dead grandfather's secret story; he felt himself was just living in an innocent spy world; thinking of this he drank a full glass of wine by once that made him a impact physically, but it made him feeling an instant relax but after that short softness, the old sorrow came up again; the night was so quiet, everything around was quiet, dead quietness; If someone break into the house right now with a pistol against his head, what would be happened? But now he is considering the possibility of that would happen.....

Telephone rang. "Hello...." Frabnky answered. "Franky, Kauffamnn speaking, how are you? Well, I ring you up just want to tell you that tomorrow morning 9:30 a.m. James Smith is calling a meeting at Madison Hall, well your class for the same hour will be taken by Vice Professor Dr. Ericmann; Well, as you know, Smith wish you could present a valuable paper from your grandfather; you know, it's so important for processing the case; do you have any idea of that?" "Well, tonight I was checking some old staffs of my grandfather and found a couple of old paper written in something like German but not exactly German; Well, I suppose I will bring it to Smith, maybe it will serve for our researching work, how do you think?" Franky said.

"It sounds wonderful, good, just bring it here tomorrow. will you do that?" Kauffamnn listened and his voice got suddenly exciting. "You bet, professor, I see uou tomorrow 9:30 a.m. Good night." "Good night, son." Kauffannn said.

"The old fox fell into my trick." Franky siad to himself.

When the wall clock knocked for 11 p.m. The door bell called. "What hell is this?" Franky was ready to go to bed. "Who is it?" he asked inside the door. "National Security

Agency, sir." the voice answered from the other side of the door. "What do you want in such a night?" "Offical business, sir.. Please open the door." Franky got no choice, he opened a slice of the door.

"Special agent Hank Dickson, sir, this is my ID and my company special agent Mike Hunt is by my side, we are here to confine your documentary, sir." The agent passed his ID through the door gap to show Franky. Franky opened widely the door and met two young agents wearing the same dark color suit; the ID printed NSA logo. "Okey, please come in." "Thank you, sir." the two guys stepped into the door. "Would you like to sit down in the living room." Franky showed them the living is in a short distance. "Thank you, sir." they followed Franky to sit on the safe one by the other. Franky sat himself on a single sofa too. "Would you please tell me what kind of paper you need?" "Oh, yes, you just had a phone communication with Dr. Kauffmann and our agency was supervising the call and our boss considered that it would be better to help you to keep that paper beforehand in order to present for tomorrow's meeting, not for bad, only for the security of national security matter." the agent said. "Sure, we will give you a receipt for that important document, sir, so please don't worry about that. besides, we have an written order signed directly by Agent James Smith, here you are, please take a look, sir." "Okey, it's no problem, allow me a couple of minutes, let me find it, okey?" "Sure, sir, just take your time."

Franky came back to the living room after about five minutes saying, "Sorry, I made mistake, the paper I just left in school, tomorrow morning the same I need attending the meeting of James Smith and I will give it directly to agent Smith, is that okey?" The two agents said something to each other's ear then said," Okey, as you say, Professor, what we cared was just the security of the saying paper; if it's not in your house, well, we will wait for tomorrow; sorry for bothering you so later." the same agent said. Franky accompanied them to the door.

"It's just like a fucking spy war....." Franky thought.

After agent's left, Franky smugglering himself out of his house by his own car rushly heading to his old house, he prepare a hand light in order to remove his box to some other places in the garden. The night job was smoothly did, nobody presured him at least. He went back home washed himself then went to bed while he was thinking how he will do for that forged paper. Rachel had promised him.

Next early morning, he found a payphone not near from his house and called Rachel urgently, Rachel listened just saying, "Don't worry, Franky, you just drop in Tony's bookstore 9 a.m. and I will prepare you that envelope before that time and you still have time to give the paper to Smith. It was 6:20 a.m.

Franky just got relaxed. He went back home to feed himself the breakfast then dressed himself well; around 8:45 a.m he drove to the downtown bookstore, when he arrived, it was about 9:10 a.m., he parked the car by the door and went into the shop, the shop was already opened since the official hour was 10 a.m. to 1 p.m. He pushed the door in and met a very thin and tall young guy was arranging books inside. "Good morning, sir, I need to see Mr. Joseph, my name is Franky." "Okey, please follow me.' the guy walked back to the register counter. "May I scan you thumb, sir?" the guy showed him a scanner and putting near Franky's hand. Franky got a little puzzled, but the guy already sacnned his right hand thumb. "Okey, you are Mr. Franky Kennedy, now I will give you the envelope." the tall guy reached his hand under the counter and took out a book sized faded color envelope to Franky. "Please be hunry, professor; Rachel told me you have to be hunry." "Oh, thank you young man." Franky rushed out the store then drove directly heading to the UV.

When Franky arrived back UV and pushed the conference room's door in, what he met was all the eyes were waiting for him, the wall coock pointed 9:45 a.m.

"Soory for being late, my alarm clock didn't ring." Franky said. "Please come in, son, we are all waiting for you." Kauffamnn said with a political smile.

Franky took the chair next to Schtok and sat himself down. "Okey, gentlemen, today Dr. Kennedy will give us the main paper for our mission. Professor, did you bring that paper?" James Smith turned his head to Franky saying. "Yes, I do." "Okey, please give it to me." "Sure, here it is. You want to take a look?" Franky drew out the paper from hid briefcase folder then handling to James.

James opened the envelope and read carefully on the old faded yellowish hard paper, it was a folded double page written antique like documentary.

"You guys want to take a look, it's written and drawing in German like but not really German letters also looking like

Yiddish language but not really like Yiddish..." James said. "Professor Schtok, would you like to take a look first?" James passed the paper first to Schtok.

Schtok put his reading glasses first then carefully studying on the paper. "It's something written in German but broked in Yiddish and Hebrew number and marks. I could understand something about 65%..." Schtok said then passed it to Kauffamnn. "65% you mean, professor Schtok....?" James asked Issac. "Yes, what is that talking about...?" "Well, something hidden in South America, but not clearly because the drawings are hard to combine with the letters." Schtok said. "Yes, it's something concerning Latin America, I found something noted in Latin letters." Kauffamnn concluded. "Dr. Franky, do you know Latin?" James asked. "Not exactly, I know every language a little, very little." Franky said.

"Okey, from now on, this documentary become to be a national property and gentlemen, you are all the members of the team; I will report it to my boss and please be aware that we are going to take a trip to South America; you guys have to be prepared, the action will be happened at any moment from now on and I think today's meeting is enough. James seemed like in a very pleasant mood.

Kauffmann left with James Smith after the meeting; Franky paced back to his office on the same floor next to the conference room; Schtok followed him into the office; "You want a cup of coffee, Dr. Schtok?" "No, thank you, I just want to have a word with you." Franky invited him to sit in front of him by his desk. "You know, Dr. Kennedy, I am here for the same mission, my question is, how did you find the paper so quickly?" "By chance, Dr.Schtok, I just found it among my father's old pages; well, James Smith liked it then I suppose it's a real McCoy."

Issac Schtok looked at Franky with a Jewish smile, then he just said: "I hope it will be useful." "Are you going to travel with us, Dr. Schtok?" "Sure, I will, don't forget I am one of the members of the team." "You know better than me, Dr. Schtok, could you tell me what we are really looking for?" "The question is, I can't tell you exactly, but something is very very important, otherwise NSA would not involve in the case." "And you are the most important key person, look, for being a friend, I suggest you just follow the order and try for not asking many questions, you know." Schtok added.

"Well, I see."

"And don't say to anybody. you know, any offical duty is of most dangeous if you don't watch your mouth." "What you just said is of James Smith's order?" Franky said. "You are a wise guy, well, I have to go back to my hotel; if you wish to talk with me, just find a payphone to make an appointment with me; Listen when you speak through the phone, don't use your true voice, put a finger under your nose, you understand me?" Schtok said in a very low tone. Issac got up then petted Franky's shoulder then left.

Franky fell into a deep thoughts.

Chapter fifteen

Franky had lunch alone in the cafeteria of the campus and gave a two hours class the same afternoon; it was near 5 p.m. when he finished the whole day long routine then he decided to visit Tony's bookstore along the way back home. He dropped in the shop and met several clients were reading around by bookstands; he neared Joseph saying in low voice: "I need to see Rachel tonight, could you arrange me an appointment?" Franky said to Joseph.

"Sure, sir. Please just to look around the books while I am going to the basement to communicate with Rachel and I would give you the asnwer immediately as soon as I got the news." Joseph said slowly. "Thank you, sir." Franky went to look around the books while Joseph went to downstairs through a side staircase. About five minutes later, Joseph showed up again and neared Franky saying "Sir, your book will be arrived at 8:30 p.m., please come here to check it out personally." "Thank you sir." Franky understood then left the house.

In order to go back home without calling more attention, Franky went to Virginia Blue restaurant not very far from the Tony's to eat a supper then went to the cafe next door to spend the rest of waiting time; nobody seemed like following him around.

Franky walked along the sidewalk window shopping different the stores and finally the night reached 8:20 p.m., then he rushed to the Tony's; the glass door hanged an 'CLOSE" sign on the back side of the glass, but a person neared the door quickly and opend it for him, it was Joseph. "Please go to the downstairs directly through the staircase overthere; Rachel is waiting for you right now." "Thank you sir." Franky followed the direction heading to the way to downstairs.

It was a big room surrounding by piles of book staffs and Rachel was sitting by a small desk by the wall, there is an extra chair in front of her.

"Welcome, Dr. Kennedy, please sit down." "Good evening, Miss Perlsztein." Franky neared the desk then sat himself down on the chair.

"I got some side information that your team is going to South America very soon, is that true?"

"You know beeter than me, lady; yes, James Smith mentioned that opportunity but I still don't know exactly what all this about?" Franky said. "Well, let me update you some information but you have to watch your mouth." Franky just looked at her and didn't say any thing. "Well, as you know, I made a forged pages to James Smith through your hand, but don't think he would be so stupid to accept it just like that; he would send it to the Lab first to make nn analysis then to decide how to do, but don't worry about that, the documentary was made under our government's high technology too. I don't think he will find out any defect, if he did, the same he will try to use part of the information to try the projected plan; look, Dr. Kennedy, what you need to do is to follow their routine and don't let him know any more details except some historical knowledge.

Well as our intellgence source shown that, the first step your team will make is to go to Falta, Cordoba, a smalltown in middle west part of Argentina; I suppose they will do it very soon, and I will accompany your route step by step but in a undercovered manner; that means you will not notice my existence along your way. Well, Dr. Kennedy, I am going to there first in a couple of days; whenever you have arrived the town just go to the direction now I am going to give you and try to contact me; can you speak Spanish? Dr.Kennedy." "Yes, I do." "Perfect, please just keep this address and name in a secret way, nobody should know it; James will work together with U.S. CIA and FBI agents there." While Rachel was handling a piece of paper slip to Keneedy.

"Then, good luck, Dr.Kennedy." Rachel said but didn't get up from the chair. "Thnak you lady." Franky got up then followed the same way back to the street. It was already 9:45 p.m. when he arrived home, the first thing he did was to note down the secret address in La Falta, Argentina.

The paper slip written:

Sr. Don Domingo
San Martin 756,
La Falta, Cordoba

Franky really didn't know what hell was going on? He made a cold shower then went to bed.

Chapter sixteen

La Falta, Codoba, Argentina, April 2012

Rachel Perlsztein took American Airlines flight left Washington D.C. heading to Miami then transited Varig non-stop directly down to Rio and arrived Bs. Aires via San Pablo, Brasil; It was not her first visit to the Capiral City of Argentina since she made several trips to this South American country with the aim of finding something she wanted, besides during her many long-stay visitations to the country she also had been visited others cities and towns more than a couple of times; she has became an expert concerning her investigating cases. This time she came here again in order to cooperate Dr. Frank Kennedy to search something important not only for Franky himself but also for her homeland.

She stayed a couple of days in Bs. Aires and visited some key persons there then traveled to La Falta, Cordoba province for preparing some jobs because she knew that James Smith and his team would be arrived this small town very soon according her official information obtained from Polish Embassy in D.C. The weather in Buenos Aires was still warm and Codoba is located about 500 and something kilometers west of the Capital City, the climate was in a little more confortable than the coastal

Federal Capital due to the level of geographcial reason. La Falta is a small town with a distance from Cordoba City, a very quiet and humble one compairing others towns.

Rachel took her simple luggage and moved in the safty house in that town, the old and not big Spanish style house called no special attention for the population living around. Polish Consulate General sited in Codoba was in charge of the function of that officail spot.

The second early morning, Rachel rode a bicycle went to the mountain root intending to find an old guy who's name was called as Julio; according her private record this man must be around 92 and he would be a person to recall some information; she spent near 20 minutes to reach the place, it was an old cottage by the mountain stream surounding by colorful bushes; the natural scene was quite pretty and plaeasant under the gentle early sunshine; she knocked the closed door and after more than a couple of minutes, a young teen boy in tobaco brown reddish hair opened the narrow wooden door looking at Rachel with somehow puzzled sights... "Hola...," the boy said. "Hola, joven, vos sabes el senor Julio Puzzlner vive aca?" "Quien es Vd.?" the boy asked. "Yo soy una amiga de su familia, me llamo Regerna, puedo verlo?" "Un momento, por favor." the boy went inside the small house.

Rachel put her bike on the road side and waiting for the boy to come out. "De donde vienes? y Vd. hablar Polaco?" the boy appeared again just questioned Rachel by the door side. "Yo vengo de Warsolvia y hablo Polaco." Rachel said.

"Un momento...." the boy went inside again. It took again near three nimutes, the boy showed up saying, "Pasa Vd. por favor." the boy just called Rachel by his hand.

Inside the house was poor and simple, a wooden bed by the right side of the wall, a couple of stools, a gas cooker and some staffs on a aged table. Rachel met an very old guy sitting by the edge of his bed.

"Buenos dias, senor Puzzlner, yo soy Regerna Puzzlner from Polonia. Rachel presented herself with a false name. "Sientese, senorita, Vd. es muy joven." the old man said. "Gracias, sneor." "Soy Capitan Julio Puzzlner, Ejercito de Polonia 1945." the old man said in a very strong voice that didn't like a man as his age.. "Oh, it's the right guy I am looking for..." Rachel said to herself.

Rachel sat herself down on a single chair near the window of the smallroom; Julio got up to serve a glass of water for the lady; he stood more or less five foot ten, old but still well built; one mightn't say he was already 92; he wore a faded apple blue short sleeves shirt and a pair of beige jean like pants. He took a chair and sitting by Rachel. "What can I do for you?" he began to speak English but with a very strong East European accent.

"Oh, I am here to visit the country and just arrived this town, my family told me we have a distance uncle who carrys the same surname as me, so I took advantage to visit you." "Which city are you from, senorita?" "Warsolvia..." Rachel said carefully. "I left there since 1947 and after so much time, now I am a local Codobes..." Julio said. "Uncle Julio, may I call you Uncle Julio?" "Call me what you want, you know, I am a very old guy, nothing is more important for me."

"Don Julio, I would like to ask you some questions, well, about this town La Falta, because I am writing a book." "Just ask me if I know something....," "Antonio, traime algo de vino...!" he shouted to the outdoor; the boy should be called as

Antonio. "Si,.. senor." the kid answered through outside. "Okey, Don Julio, you arrived La Falta in 1947, is that right?" "Yes, I did; it was around 1947 or two months earlier." "Do you know there was a fameous Hotel called Hotel Ida?"

"May be...? But I don't quite remember, it was around 1953, I was still young, 33 years old, I worked in a mechanic works about half a block of a big Hotel, I couldn't remember the name, you know, there were a lot of tourist hotels in this town, many tourists on and back; well, I just remind one thing, there was a very millionare like couple arrived that hotel and stayed near a week, because during that week a lot of visitors came with very expensive cars; it was like a festival..." "Do they spoke English?" "No..., no,...no..., they were speaking German..." Julio said while he sipped mere mouth of wine. "How did you know they were German?" "Because I could speak German and English beside my home language." Julio said. "Why did you ask me such a question?" "Because I am writing a novel concerning the life between Europe and South America after the War II." Rachel said. "Hummm...., it would be interesting..." "Do you know this man?" Rachel showed Julio a black and white yellowish faded picture showing a guy in Germany military uniform in his early fifites or less... "I don't know this guy...!" Julio peeked the picture then said definitively. "Don. Julio, could you tell me somthing about your own story? Did you say you were serving in Polish Army?" "Yes, I did. I was a Capitan officer of Polish Army in 1946 and I spent one year in Nazi's concentration sited at Auchwitz; but I survived in that year." "Oh, it was so interesting, how did you get survived from that death camp?"

"Because I was working as a 'capo' for supervising the Jews." Julio said while he was enjoying his wine. "After 1945, what did you do?" "I flew to Argentina through Spain." "La falta was your first stop?" "No, I lived in Buenos Aires's Jewish town for near half year then I moved to Codoba after 1947. Why did you ask me such a lot of my personal history? young lady." "Because one of our family member once was talking about your history." "You are a lier, you are not from our family either; but anyway, I don't care you are of CIA, FBI or even MOSSAD, because I had died once in Buenos Aires..." Julio laughed. "Oh..., that's so interesting, Don Julio, why did you die once in Buenos Aires?" "Sure, I did, but young lady, I am not going to tell you the story this time; But it was true, I did die in Ramos Mejia Hospital in Bs. Aires in 1987 but I survived at German Hospital three days later, then I came to Codoba again." "Muy bien, ese es todos, por favor, senorita, vayase, yo tengo que hacer algo en particular." Julio began to speak Spanish again and he got up to see Rachel off.

Rachel left the place through the same bike way that morning, it was about 9:40 a.m. She went back to the safty house and passed the whole voice cellphone recording into electronic file.

The same afternoon, she hired a cab and asked the driver to drive her to Ida Hotel. "Senorita, ya no hay Hotel Ida aca." the tacheno said. "Entonce qual es mas viejo y grande hotel en La Falta?" "Bueno, hay un hotel se llma Hotel Juan D. Peron puede serera Hotel Ida, pero no estoy muy seguro." the old Codobes driver said in very heavy Codoba province accent.

"Muy bien, senor, por favor llevarme a este Hotel.' "Esta bien, senorita, como Vd. dice." the cab begen to run. It only took near ten minutes around the small country town road. and arriving an very ancient but elegant masion style hotel, it was looking luxury but in a very noble and cultural taste.

Rachel got off from the old Taxi after paid fare and tip to the old guy. "Gracias...., hermanita.....," the tachero said.

Rachel first took the full view of that old but mansion like elegant and noble taste hotel using her smartphone then heading to the doorway of the hotel.

The Hotel was in a very Argentine province country fasion, simple, clean, elegant; the lobby was not so bright but big enough under soft tango music floating in the air. An elder well dressed male clerk was working quietly behind the long wooden counter....

"Buenos Dias, senor." Rachel greeted the guy as soon as she approaching the counter. "May I help you, senorita?" the clerk answered the blonde young lady when he realized that the vistor was a foreigner. "I am a reporter from Europe and I am a book writer too. What I need is to have some information of your Hotel; may I speak to your public relation manager?" Rachel said while she handled a forged name card to the receptionist.

"Sure, madam, would you please waite for a minutes on the sofa over there and our ground floor manager will be seeing you in a couple of minutes, please..." the guy with a thick mustache showed gentlely the direction on his left side. "Sure, sir. thank you." Rachel looked over the place walking to the sofe about ten meters in didtance.

"Senorita, Jorge Lopez a su ordenes. Soy genente de la plata baja." A middle sized fat Codobes in his early fourties presented by Rachel's side. "Oh, mucho gusto, senor Lopez, me llamo Christina Jackson, la periodista de la Revista Hoteles & Turismos de la Inglandera; Quicia alguna informacion sobre la historia de este famoso Hotel en Codoba, aca esta mi tarjeta por favor." "Tanto gusto a conocerte, senorita Jackson, solamente decirme con que puedo servirte?"

"Quicia saber alguna noticia sobre el Hotel during el ano 1953?" "Es muchos tiempos atras, senorita..., no es verdad?" "Exactamente, senor Lopez, es sobre las noticias de este paraja?" Rachel showed Jorge an old picture on which a middle sized man in short hair in his eraly fifties wearing gray suit and beside him a short young lady also in short hair standing by him; they dressed quite modren according to that period of time.

Jorge took the picture in hand and studied for several seconds then he said' "No creo, yo puedo conocer a este paraja porque este image es muchos mas viejos que mi edad, no es asi?" "Senor Lopez, no hay una persona mas viejo de edad y todovia puede levantar alguna memorias para este photo, por ejembro, una persona que ya tiene mas que 75 anos."

"Tenemos un carpentero ya esta jubilado se llama Jose Gomez, el tstuve trabajando aqui mas o menos durante este anos; Pero el ya no esta mas travajado aqui..." "Este senor ya esta muerdo?" "No se, todavia; miras, el ultima vez yo lo vi era dos anos atras pero en un proble unos 20 kilometros de aca." Jorge said. "Puede decime la direccion?" "Si, como no, pero yo no puedo a securote este senor todavia esta vivo?" "No importa, Vd. solamente damelo el lucal y el nombre de la calle es bastante." Rachel said anxiously.

"Vd. puedes decirme por que quiers buscar este tipo?" "Por una tema historico que quisir publicar sobre una revista muy importante de la Europa." Rachel said.

"Bueno, si es asi, con mucho gusto. por favor dames unos minutos." Jorge left the sofa heading to the lobby counter. He took off the tube of the counter telephone and began to make calls....

Rachel spend near more than five minutes waiting for his return. The middle sized well built dark Codobes came back with a commercial smile saying:" Aca esta el direcion de este senor." he handled a piece of small paper with the hotel's logo to Rachel.

> **Jose Gomez**
> **Cuenca 346**
> **Villa de Silvia**
> **Codoba**

"Donde esta Villa de Silvia? Senor Lopez?" "Si Vd. va tomar un taxi, mas o menos, uno los 20 minutos puede llegar alli." "Pero, yo no te asercuguro, si Vd puede contra a este senor, el mejor manera es vaya a comisaria a aveiqual?" Jorge said. "Muchismos gracias, senor Lopez, Vd. es muy amable.' "El gusto es mio, senorita.' Lopez said gently.

Rachel Perlsztein came out of the Hotel Juan D. Peron was around 3:10 p.m., she waved a cab by the roadside decided to visit the old guy directly. "She went onto the cab and gave the paper to show the driver saying," Vamos por alla." "Como no, senorita." The driver pressed his pad down heading to the place speedy. Codoba's green mountainous scene was great along the both sides of the car windows. It took no less than 20 minutes as Lopez had said, the cab left the province main road and turned into a small village town, there was a road sign written: "Bienviendos A Villa Silvia" "This is the place." Rachel thought.

The cab went to travel among the small side streets and finally arrived to an old and poor house, the house plate written "Cuenca 346. Rachel got off the cab after paying the fare. It was around 3;50 p.m.

Rachel neared the narrow house door amd found a old style electric bell on the right side of the wall, she preseed twice. Somebody answered the door after a couple of minutes, "A quien buscar Vd. senorita."

"Oh, buenas tardes, quisia ver el senor Jose Gomez por favor."

"Quien es Vd,?" the country woman in her middle sixties began to study Rachel up to down.

"Soy la amiga de el senor Jorge Lopez de el Hotel Juan D. Peron." Rachel lied. "Pero mi marido no esta ahora.' "A donde puedo buscarlo, senor?" "No se, por favor anda a el bar esta en la esquina a veces Vd. puede colocarlo; porque el siempre anda a este horas para tomar alguno copas de vino con los amigos o vecinos, que se yo..."

"Muchas gracias, senor Gomez, Vd es muy amable." "No hay de que." the old woman closed the door back.

Rachel walked back about one block and met a cafe bar located just at the street corner; it was an very ancient traditional bar, a narrow door with a couple of wide windows but without glasses, a faded metal made sign was attaching on the cement made wall with Coca Colas's matto but in the year 60s fasion.

Rachel stepped into the bar, several square wooden tables were occupied by near dozon country guys; there was a middle sized wooden counter back to the rear wall, a middle aged beard guy in his late fourties was attending the bar.

"Quisia ver el senor Jose Gomez, por favor." Rachel neared the bartendet asking about the person she wanted to meet.

"Alla esta, el viejo flaco con bigotes es Jose Comez." the bartender showed his mouth towards an old thin guy was drinking with the rest three jerks by the table closed to the window.

"Gracias, senor." The bartender just answered with his head.

Rachel approached the guy saying:" Senor Jose Gomez?" "Quiens es Vd.?" Jose looked at the blonde foreign young lady with very puzzled sights.

"Oh, senor Gomez, soy parte de el senor Jorge Lopez de el Hotel Juan D. Peron; el me recommendo a ver Vd. para saber algunas cosas de el pasado de este ciudad; soy una periodista de la Revista de Hoteles y Turismos de el Europa; vengo especialment a visitar esta hermosa ciudad; puedo invitar a Vd. para tomar algo y chalarmos algo y yo te voy a pagar a Vd. alguno dineros..." Jose listend then said, "Muy bien, no hay problem, pero vamos a la mesa vecina, puede ser?" "Por

supuesto, senor Gomez, entonces, vamos a sentar a esta mesa."
Rachel movedherself to the next table and Jose followed her too.

"Que va a tomar Vd. senor Comez?"

"Bueno, dame otro whisky doble..." Jose was already a
little drunk. The bartender came down to the table to take
the order, he did mozo's job too. "Cuandos platas Vd. me va
dar?" "Bueno, tengo un par de preguntas, buenos me voy darle
20 pesos tambien?" Rachel said. "Si, pero, 20 pesos con otro
whysky doble..." "Como Vd. dice.' Rachel promised. "Muy
bien, entonces, digame Vd. si conocia este paraja? En que ano
y en donde?; digame la verdad."

Rachel showed Jose the couple's photo. Jose took the picture
then studied a little saying, "Si, pero, en muchos anos atras..."

"En que ano?"

"Mas o menos en el ano 1953.'

"En donde?"

"En el hotel Ida de entonces..."

"Te hablarba con ellos?"

"No, no pudo porque ello son gentes muy muy importantes.'

"Quien era vos?"

"Yo era un capentero joven."

"Cuando anos tenia Vd. entonces?"

"25 anos."

"In 1953, Vd. tinia 25 anos."

"Si, senorita.'

"Cuandos tiempos la paraja vivia en esta hotel?"

"No me recuerdo muy bien, que se yo, puede ser unos thres
a cuatro dias." Jose said.

"Cuandos anos Vd. tiene ahora?"

"Tengo 74 anos."

"Muy bien, sneor Gomez, buenos, aca tiene Vd. 20 pesos y me voy compra otro whisky doble para vos." Rachel put a 30 pesos bill on the table. Jose made an innocent smile.

All the conversation between Jose and herself had already wired on to her cellphone memory card.

Rachel called a cab to send her back to her safety house in the uptown of the Codoba City. It was 6 p.m. already.

Chapter seventeen

La Ciudad de Codoba was consdered as the secondary most popular city in Argentina and its deep Spanish culture also Catholic religion bathed flavor made any foreign tourist a breathtaking suprise and somehow a kind of pleasant feeling; it's so quiet and peaceful country completely outside of Buenos Aires influences; green highland surrounding the modern part also the old area of a paradise like land far away from Rio de la Plata. The beautiful ancient Catholic churches with cooper made high gate and Chinese forbidden city type door knocker which was made as a lion holding a ring in his mouth on the both sides of the high door that just could drive your imagination back to middle age of European era. South American quietness and culture expressions could not easy translate to any language; you just need to feel as a tourist.

Rachel was walking along the wide street of Codoba City on her way to visit Padre Eriquel Acevedo, a Catholic Father who was in charge of an huge downtown church.

The elegant and Roma artistic style beautiful church stood remarkably in the downtown Ciudad de Cordoba; it was so evident antique jewlery like construction located among hundreds buildings in this hermosa mountain city.

Rachel stepped into the church first to greet the Virgen's beautiful standing figuer then followed the left side pathway intending to find the Archbishop's main office; an elegant young prist in his long balck dress neared Rachel and gently asking Rachel's nature of visit? Rachel named Archbishop Enquel Acevedo, the young gent nodded the head then led her to follow his way to the Father's office.

They walked along soft red carper leading the way to the main office and Italian styled art works decorated with gold and some colorful stones highlighting the greatness of Roman Catholic history and power; they finally arrived a deep and safe place on teh second floor of the church through an ancient birdcage like elevator.

There was a dark red coated cooper made door by the right side of the red carpeted corridor, the gentle and soft palace like lights illuninating the peaceful pathway. The young prist knocked twice the door then pushed the door in smoothly inviting Rachel to go in showing his smiling eyes.

"Gracias, padre." Rachel said to the young man then walked in.

What she met was a middle siazed elder gentleman in his later seventies wearing the red and black combined not very formal Catholic Archbishop's dress standing by a brown red color single sofa decorated by gold and black wood standings. The old man was wearing a kind and affection like smile receiving Rachel's arriving. Rachel walked gently neared the prist and softly lowed a little her knee before to kiss the Father's hand.

"Welcome to Cordoba, Miss Rachel Perlsztein." the Father holding Rachel's hand and led her to sit with him on a long sofa by the left side of the room. A big sized Miquel Angeler style huge painting was hanging on upper part of the wall.

"Your Eminence, it's so nice to meet you." Rachel said respectfully. "Tanto gusto, Sta. Rachel Perlsztein." Enriquel said. "The Consul of your Consulate General in Cordoba Mr. Joseph Halgonovsky phoned me this morning concerning your visiting; he is my friend for many years in here Cordoba; Anything you need in this city just tell me..." The Father said with a warm smile but his wise and smart sights penetrating through his lens of the gold flamed glasses that made Rachel feeling his great power. "Thank you, your Eminence; what I need is to know if you could give me some historical information about this man?" Rachel drew out a small book sized faded yellowish black and white photo showing a black uniformed German military guy in his middle thirties." she handling the picture carefully to Acevedo's hand.

The Archbishop received the old photo and took a look very carefully saying: "Yes, he was late SS Brigadefuhrer Hagen Duetch; he was here around 1953 or 1954 when I was still working as a teen helper in this church." Enriquel said.

"What a good memory you have, your Eminence." Rachel answered. "I remember this picture because I have been an investigator over this part of history." Acevedo said.

"Would you also tell me if you have any knowledge concerning this picture?" Rachel showed the Father the couple's faded black and white photo. The Father just peeked it saying: "Oh, it's a fameous picture used to publish on world wide gossiper macazine; I can't give any credit fo it; I can't say it's a fake picture neither, but I have no any knowledge about its real identity." the Archbishop said.

"What do you mean is that this picture has nothing to do with this City, your Reminence?" "I have no comment on it." "As I have heard that La Falta arrived a lot of Germany immigrants after 1945, is that true?" "Yes, it was true, not only in La falta, the whole Cordoba province, the whole Argentina even the whole South America, everywhere..."

"Miss Perlsztein, I welcome you to visit me every afternoon after 4 p.m. and I would tell you more details; but today please allow me to make an excuse, I need a short nap because I am feeling a little tired; Whenever you wish to come please make a phonce call to my secretary previously; you may withdrow my name card from the fraont desk as soon as you are leaving this church." Enriquel got up slowly while he gave his hand to Rachel. "Thank you for receiving me, your Reminence, thank you for your kindness." Rachel said. "You are very welcome, young lady." the Father began to walk heading slowly to the room inside.

Rachel left the church and waved a cab by the wide pavement to ask the cab driver to send her back to her safety house.

It was near 5 p.m., she made herself confortable after a shower then sat by her desk thinking detailly about the conversation between the Father and her; She didn't really believing in the Archbishop's words. She rose her desk phone tube and made a phone call to Professor Eminio Luna, a history professor of Universidad de Cordoba. The professor invited her to visit his house located at the westean part of Cordoba City;

the appointment was setting for 8 p.m. The street number was Santa Cruz de la Sierra 1783

Rachel found something in the fridge, a samwitch of jamon y queso and a small galss of vino tinto; she feed herself before to visit Eminio Luna.

Rachel took a cab outside her place asked the driver to send her to the address nated on a slice of paper; the silence tachero speedy the car runing among the night peaceful streets and only spent near 15 minutes, they arrived the correct strret number, Rachel paid the fare and tip before getting off.

It was a common residence like house on a narrow side street, she pressed the door bell and met a short and thin local Cordobes receiving her by the door with a gentle smile. "Senorita Perlsztein, welcome to our home, please come in;

I would like to introduce my family to you.'

"Pleased to meet you, senor Luna."

"The pleasure is mine, Por favor, comeing in." Luna led Rachel heading to the house doorwaya couple of meters away.

"Ella es mi senora Marta, mi hijo Ronando, 16 y mi hija Rosita 12." Luna presented his small family to Rachel in his small living room. Rachel said hello to everyone in the living; then Luna invited her to go into his studying room for details. The studying room was surrounding by three full wall length book cases fulling of the books, it was really looking like a professor's working world. Luna invited Rachel to sit by his desk just in front of him; Marta came in and served them Argentine mate tea then left.

There was a small garden by the window of the studying room. The air was quite smooth and nice. "Que puedo servir, senorita Perlsztein?" Luna said, he was wearing a semi new button down gray shirt with thin darker strips, his heavy shortsighted glasses and thick mustacher made him looking much older than his age.

"Yes, Professor Luna, I met Archbishop this afternoon and showed him a couple of pieces of old photos and he only recognized one of them, the picture of the SS Major General Hagen Duetch and concerning the other picture he said he had no any knowledge about it." Rachel opened the chat box.

"Yes, along my near two decades investigating over the modern Argentine history especially on this part of our homeland also on Patagonia, I have been written several books resulting my long time works and I also cooperated with many fameous local and European historians for exchanging our studyings and sincerely I couldn't agree many of the bishop's views since he used to be a very influential person on politics also he did many joint works with the former military government during the dirty war and that was why he could be nominated and elected as the bishop for our City. if you wish to believe in him better to believe in Devil." "What you just said meaning that the bishop is not a correct historian?" Rachel asked. "He is just a dirty religious rat, forgive my word." Luna said. "Would you suggest me to go on my investigation down to Patagonia?" "As you know La Falta connection had directly related to Patagonia connection." Luna said. "Professor Luna, could you tell me as your opinion that the couple on the picture I just showed you had been really staying a short time in La Falta?" Rachel asked. "Look, this question would be discovered 30 or 40 years later from now on since you know it's been a very sensitive theme; well, that means under the superpower's influences, the question is not allowed to be very certainly discussed; so, if the answer is yes or it's no, it not really important any longer because it has been gone with time, yes?" Luna stopped a mere while then continued to say:" But, the guy you showed me on the other photo is right now a very confidential case and, Miss Perlsztein, my good advise is that try not to touch it too deep because it's too dangerous under certain circumstances, you know...." Luna sipped a mouthful mate tea.

"But, as you see, I am under an offical mission of the Polish Government." Rachel said. "But, the Yankee and Moises are two very strong power; you should to avoid their united forces." Luna said. "Is that true that Hagen Duetch was a Jew?"

"Yes, he was a German Jew and afterwords turnned to be an American in 1964 and he died in 1967 in Virginia." "But how could he raised to be a SS Major General at the end of the War II?" Rachel said.

"The same Adolf Ericmann was also a Jew but he was quility for millions of lives in Aushwitz and he was only a Colonel." Luna said, he stopped a little went on saying:" But Hagen had a better fate after the War; he enjoyed almost 16 years long good life in Patagonia; well, I don't want to mention with who he was doing his business, but I know that your purpose on this trip is to find something he did in Patagonia, right?" Luna said. "Not exactly, Professor Luna; yes, to find Hagen's ruins is one of my aim but most importantly, I would like to know the truth about what he really did to my Dad that caused my Dady's later miserable life in Polonia." "How's your father right now?" "He died in Wasawvia in 1982 when I was only 4." Rachel said. "Oh, I am sorry for hearing that." Luna said. "Miss Perlsztein, you still want to asure the couple's fate?" "Yes, I would like to find some positive details since it's not so important for the case I am looking for now; but anyhow, it would be helpful in anyway..." Rachel said. "For my knowledge, you are a senoir inverstigator for modern history of University of Warsaw, is that right?"

"Yes, I am."

"Okey, good. if you would like, there is a retired singer who's name is Suzenen Meagele now is living in somewhere in San Pablo, Brasil; she was very popular during 90s both in Brasil and Argentina and she is having a DNA relationship with Joseph Meagele, now she is about 52. Well, you could go there to visit her through your Cosulate General in San Pablo and I am sure you could find something you need." Luna suggested Rachel. Rachel listened Luna's word first she got a little shock then she intended to control a little bit then saying: "Oh, it might a good idea; I will think about it."

"Look. Miss Perlsztein, it's so late now and as you know the City is not safe during the night; Our house is not big enough but we own a guest room, you could pass the night here if you don't mind; otherwise, I could ride you home." Luna said. "Don't worry, professor, I could call a cab to get home since the distance is quite short." Rachel said. "Okey, if the distance is not long, then I suppose there will be no any problem; Well, Miss Perlsztein, you could reach me easily in my University, I even give class everyday there; Just come to visit me anytime you wish; I would asisitant you as most I can."

"Thank you, Professor, you are very kind." Rachel quitted the short man then took a cab back home, it even took less then 15 minutes with less traffics along the way. She took a shower then did a homework for the same day's results.

Chapter eighteen

San Pablo, La Ciudad de Brasil, April 2012

The next morning she got up and decided to take a trip to San Pablo, Brasil; she called Consul General in Cordoba and expressed the idea, the Consul booked a round trip ticket for her with diplomatic ID and the trip was scheduled on the same day 3 p.m; what she needed to do was to wait an hour before at the Cordoba Airport, the ticket will be arrived in her hand. through Consulate agent.

Rachel made a simple arrangement then took a cab heading to the airport with her dark reddish leather briefcase. The trip will be taken about four and half hours from Cordoba to San Pablo via Buenos Aires.

San Pablo is a metropolitan, a southern coastal City not very far from Rio de Jeneiro; it's a great city mixed beautiness of Chicago and New York but with South America hot and spicy flavor; hundreds of Skyscrapers, elegant Catholic ancient churches, rivers crossing under bridges, super up to date highways; romantic streets with trees, gardens, sea coast and highland, mixed colors of people, so called 'Cafe con Leche'; everythig that only belonging to this hot and sexy great City; its wideness and pride, everything.......

Rachel checked in a midder class hotel called Hotel Do Santos located on uptown of S.P. City after about 5 hours flying; it was about 9 p.m. locat time and she connected Joham Nicovsky, the Consul General of Poland sited in San Pablo who came to Raches's hotel one hour after and they had a meeting in the Hotel's cafe on the thrid floor.

Rachel told Nicovsky her nature of visiting and the tall and handsome young Consul promised her to set an appointment with the former singer Sunenen Meagele for the next day. Joham gave his contact name card to Rachel then left the Hotel.

Rachel had a cold shower then went to the 5th floor salon to watch a short dancing show also a couple of songs by a fat middle aged negro lady singer, the song was singing in Portuques but Rachel enjoyed it.

A thin and tall Brasilian mixed blooded guy in his middle thirties, well dressed in white suit neared Rachel's table, "Excuse me madam, ABIN, may I ask you a couple of questions?" the guy said in very strong Brasil accent English. "What's ABIN, who are you?" Rachel got suprised. "Agencia Brasileira De Inteligencia, lady, a routine check." "Oh, yes..." Rachel changed completely her mood. "May I see your passport, madam?" the man said in gentle but offical manner. "My passport is still remaining in the front counter; this is my name card; I am the member of Polish Ministry of Foreign Affairs." Rachel passed a forged name card to the guy. "If it's so, sorry for bothering you and have a nice evening.' the guy left. "Oh, another police country." Rachel said to herself. She lost interest to go on watch then went back to her room.

She got up at 8 a.m. the next morning and first ordered the room service breakfast and 20 minutes later, the room door knocked, she went to answer the door, a black young waiter was waiting by the door with the cart, his smile liked San Pablo's sun that relaxed a little Rachel's mind. "Bom dia, madam." the young boy said. "Bom dia, joven, pasa por favor."

The young guy served the food on the table then ready to leave. "Tomala Vd." Rachel gave him some bucks for a tip. "Muitos obligados, madam." he left with a sunny smile.

When Rachel was just enjoying her breakfast, her cellphone rang, the Polish Consul General called her for setting an appointment for 2 p.m. and he promised her to come to the Hotel to pick Rachel up and he will personally present her to the singer. Rachel appreciated his attention.

After the breakfast, she sat by the hotelroom window forcusing the far distance sea coast and trying to put all together some data she collected in Europe before taking this trip to America; she wrote some details in Polish language about the cases she needed to discover in South America. She opened the book sized notebook which was looking like her grandmon's era old diary for not calling attention, all in handrwitting nothing electronics. Well, as she had written: 1971 + 1979 J. M. S. P wolfgonggerhard embudasartes Hundreds of lines like that.

It was the only way she herself could understand.

At the mean time, she tried to review in mind that person's life story as she had studied in University of Warsowvia; when she would meet the former fameous singer she would have some idea to find more details she would need for her mission.

Rachel came to Virginia first then down to Soth America not only for her offical mission but also for her family affairs since her Grandpa was Hagen Duetch's enemy also one time been partner; they were all dead men but the legacy goes on.....

She was thinking of Dr. Franky Kennedy, a poor innocent devil who is still living in the stupid present.

Rachel spent the whole morning closed in her room studying the old references intending to find some new clue that might be useful for her next step.

She called a room service simple lunch to feed herself, then took a shower, a short nap and ready to meet the past-time singer.

Around 1:20 p.m. Joham Nicovsky called from the Hotel's lobby counter saying her car is just parking by the doorway ready to go with her to meet the appointment with Miss Sunenen Meagele.

Rachel had already dressed up as a noble young lady, she took her briefcase rushed down to the ground floor and meet the young Consul by his car side. Nicovsky dressed in his dark gray middle season suit in a very elegant manner; he opened the passenger door for Rachel then went to sit behind the wheel.

"Miss Perlsztein, we only need 15 minutes to arrive the singer's up-town office." Joham said. "And along the way, you could enjoy the breathtaking wonderful City scene." he added. "Sure, I will. Mr. Consul General." Rachel replied.

Nicovsky rode his car first passing a piece of romantic beachside then heading onto the highway to go to 2628 Paulista Avenue.

They reached the doorway of the building almost near 2:00 p.m.

It was a nice sunny day.

Licovsky got off the car then opened the door for Rachel, the porter neared Joham to take the keys for parking the car.

Then they went into the luxury resident like building to get the three ways elevator to go to the 16th floor.

"Did you enjoy the trip, Miss Perlsztein?" "Yes, I did, but somebody was following us along the way..." Rachel said.

"Do you suppose so?" "Yes. I guess that but I am not so sure..." "You know, Brasilian male guy used to presure beautiful girl likes you along the way.." Joham said.

Rachel just tried to regular her appearance and said nothing.

It took just several seconds to arrive the correct floor, the door opened they just met another door secured with metal bars on the otherside of the corridor; Joham pressed the bell as soon as they neared the door; a dark suit young lady came to answer the door with a gentle smile.

"Good afternoon, My name is Nicovsky, we have an appointment with Miss Meagele at 2 p.m." "Oh, please just come in, Miss Meagele is expecting for you both." the young girl touched a hidden button then the door opened suddenly.

They just met a full floor wide office like suite in a very luxury decorations. The full length huge glass covering almost the full wall of the other side forcusing the far image of San Pablo coastal beach in a very far distance.

The suite was divided in several rooms but the separations were all of transperant design except a couple of unseen parts. The young lady led them to sit on a confortable long sofa and served drinks in a couple of minutes.

At this moment, a middle aged but very fasion dressed beauty appeared from one side door of the wall. She was about five foot five, pure white but reddish skinned, green blue eyes, she wore one inch and half common high heel colorful leather shoes combining her multicolor lady's dress too. Her appearence made Rachel and Joham a breathtaking motion.

"Welcome to my office, Mr. Consul General and the young lady." she was speaking a strong German accent Brasilian English. Joham neared her to kiss her right side cheek also presented Rachel to her at the same time.

They sat all together confortably then began the chat box.

Rachel was presented as an European magazine reporter coming to San Pablo to interview the fameous singer especially. Miss Meagele's gentle amd smart smile showed her quality of world class looking. After several polite cross conversation, Rachel began to ask Meagele some sensible questions.

"Is Meagele your true surname, Madam?"

"Sure, it is."

"Is Joseph Meagele your grandfather?"

"Oh, he is nothing to do with our family, they were from the north of Germany and we were from the south of Germany."

"You lived in Buenos Aires for near ten years, is that right?"

"Sure, it was, because I did sucessful show business there during 90s."

"Have you been often the town Embu das Artes?"

"Only once, it's a popular tourist site after 1979." Meagele said. Joham eyed Rachel to watch a little her mouth.' Miss Meagele maintained her noble and kind smile along all the time; she asked the young lady to bring two pieces of her artistic picture to present to the two guys and put her innitial personally.

Rachel asked her permission to make a picture with her through her cellphone; the attractive former actress made two with Rachel. Nicovsky quitted Meagele and left with Rachel about 40 minutes later.

On the back ride, Joham suggested Rachel to visit Consulate with him in order to exchange some points and promised Rachel to have dinner at night for discussing more details, Rachel didn't say no.

The Nicovsky rode Rachel back to his office located a place very close to the seaside.

Joham arrived to the doorway of the Consulate office house located on the avenue around the seaside coast; it was a three floor mansion kind nice house and the Polish white and red horizontal bicolor national flag was flying on the stand of the second floor. Rachel felt so good when she saw her homeland's color.

Nicovsky led Rachel to go to his main office which was loacted on the second floor through the one of the three lines elevators. The office was designed in a very offical fasion; the wide transperant window was forcusing onto the seacoast in a very close distance. The Consul General first instruduced Rachel to his private secretary Sophia, a middle aged Polish lady then led her to sit with him in a special room inside in order to have private meeting with Rachel; Sophia knew that once the Consul went into that room just means he would'nt be bothered.

Joham served personally coffee for Rachel, then they sat confortablely face to face on a middle sized round table to discuss the case confidentially. "What I want to know is wheather the singer had direct DNA connection with Joseph Meagele?"

"For this point, I could tell you yes,"

"Do you have any proof?" Rachel asked.

"Just information through our direct intellgence upper chief."

"Okey, wrong or right, that's enough; but that doesn't important."

"The important point is, did Hagen Duetch had connections with Joseph Meagele before 1979?"

"Since I know, there was a chain connections among San Pablo, Busnos Aires, Cordoba, Tucuman, Misiones, Paraguay, Patagonia even as north to Salta province of Argentina..."

Rachel added.

"And Montevideo, Uruguay too." Nicovsky said.

"As you know, Mr. Consul; we have to investigate many things in this area for our homeland; but anyway, we have to wait the U.S. mission team to arrive to Buenos Aires and to follow them through undercovered manner to find some common points; But the very important point is that nobody has to know our existence, sir." Rachel said.

"I truly understand that; Be sure, Miss Perlsztein, our Polish intellgence network through South America will do our best to cooperate you to fullfill the mission and we will do our full support everywhere over the South America territory, you know."

"That's what I really want.' Rachel said.

"So, the main role is Hagen Deutch and not the couple on the old picture." Nicovsky said.

"You are 200% right." Rachel answered. Nicovsky got up and went to the side wall, first removed a wall picture of a painting then opened the safe box on the wall; he took out a thick elevelope then closed everything back. he came back to the table and handled the envelope to Rachel saying: "Miss Perlsztein, there are six pieces of real and offical Polish passports with different names and data but all attarched your photos in order to protect you in any emergency; you could use any one to pass any migeration control around the world; they are all real diplomatic passports insurred by our government; just keep them well, yes." Nicovsky said.

Rachel nodded and kept them into her purse. "And whenever James Smith, Issac Schtok, Kauffmann and Kennedy arrived to Bs. Aires or any City of Argentina, our diplomatic agency in Argentina will update you at once and will support you in everywhere of the Argentine territory; this is an offical order from our Presidency House in Wasawvia, you know." Nicovsky said seriously.

"Yes, sir." Rachel said.

"But as you know, Mr. Nicovsky. What James Smith's investigating route is not the same as ours." Rachel added. "Why did you say so?" "Because their idea is completely basing on the source of Franky Kennedy's family and besides, they really still believing in the couple's South America theory."

"Yes, maybe you are right, but do you think Issac Schtok who is having the same idea on the case?" Nicovsky asked. "Well, he is from Mossad and he is carrying more or less the same idea as ours, but we can let him to advance too much, because that will be against our homeland's interest. Rachel said.

"But please do not undervalue Mossad's great power cross the world." "I never think so, sir. Isreal is a close partner with the U.S. but on this case; Mossad will do its own way."

"And please don't undervalue SIDE Argentina's great influence either." "Yes, I know, but they might be smart but not so advanced in technology." Rachel said. "Don't forget Argentina used to be a pro-Nazis and Facist country up to now." "Don't worry, sir. I will try to fullfill our mission." Rachel said. "So, what you mean is that we have to concentrate in Hagen Duetch not the couple, is that right?" the Consul said. "This is our government's indication." Rachel said.

"Okey. Miss Perlsztein, tonight you will dine with me but outside this office; you know, I am not quite sure my office is wired by the local government; besides, people used to say our Polish people could betray to each other often." "That's Jew's opinion on us; I don't think so." Rachel said. "How many empolyees do you have?" "About two dozons or less." "Do you think they are all tridors?" "I don't think so, but we never know, two or three are enough to ruin everything." Nicovsky said. "Yes, money talks."

Rachel and Nicovsky left together around 5 p.m. Nicovsky planned to show Rachel a part of the City before sunset and after that they went go to somewhere to have dinner also to discuss details with security.

They drove to the beachside of the City and chose a cafe-restaurant style not very noticeable shop to sit by the outdoor table under a huge green and yellow parasol.

"Here is the better place." Nicovsky said. "Do you think so? Nobody is following us? Don't forget we are in Brasil." Rachel said. "Well, I am not sure, but it's better than any diplomatic reception party where used to have a lot of spies." "Well, it's normal since diplomacy is intellgence as you know." Rachel said. "Not completely, for example, I used to be a professional diplomat since I began my career; But some guys they were old spies and afterwards they changed their runway to be a diplomat; for those guys diplomacy is the same as intellgence." Nicovsky said. "Well, Mr. Consul, let's begin; would you mind I ask you question one after the other? "Of course, just shoot me." the young Consul said.

"Do you have any knowledge that Hagen Deutch had been in here San Pablo before 1963?" "Well. my knowledge is according the file's record, yes, he did in 1962 no later." "Did he had contact with Brasilian government then?" "I suppose yes, but not directly." "You mean secretly?" "Yes, it was." Nicovsky sipped a mouthful soft drink saying. "Did he met Joseph Meagele?" "Yes, he did. At that time Meagele was working for a business company as a manager but before December of that year 1960." "Did Hagen visied Buenos Aires, Asusion even Santiago de Chile?" "Yes, he did, not only once. He even lived in a short time in Tucuman, Misiones, Salta; well, the most time he spent were in Patagonia, you know." "You mean he spent near more than 15 years in Patogonia?" "At least as I studied the record, he lived in Argentina between 1946 to 1963." Nicovsky said.

"Well, with the couple in the picture?" "Let's put the couple out of the question; the couple is not our point; just let the world to justify it; our country is now only concerning the correct map that Hagen made during his lifetime, you know, it's our main point and we don't hope any U.S. concern or Israel concern and less the Argentine concern; we need to work as a cold snake under everything, then we could achieve our goal." Nicovsky was speaking liked a specialist for the case.

"Very good, sir. Do you have any update information about when the U.S. team will be arrived to Buenos Aires?" "I think they would do it very very soon within three to five days, but I am not sure they would first come to Buenos Aires or Cordoba province; this time when you go back, better take another route; first to fly to Chile and enter the country with one of you new passport then go to La Falta again with the same new one; you know, with this manner, you could avoid Argentine SIDE's double record and try not forget your new name.' "Yes, I will do it; it's not my first mission, I did a Russian operation four years ago when I was 30 and I fullfilled the mission alone." Rachel said with a light smile. "That's good, Miss Perlsztein."

They went to eat the dinner in another restaurant and watched a hotel show in a coastal tourist Hotel.

It was 10:30 p.m. when Nicovsky rode back Rachel to her hotel. "So long, Miss Perlsztein. You better take a plane to go to Chile tomorrow and you could connect our Embassy or Consulate in everywhere of Argentina and remember that, you are under the full support by our homeland; good luck." Nicovsky said.

"Thank you so much, Mr. Consul General. I will see you."

"Sure.' Nicovsky got on his car and disappeared into the darkness.

Chapter nineteen

Santiago de Chile, April 2012

Lan Chile flight No. 424 arrived Santiago International Airport from San Pablo at 3:20 p.m. local time. The plane just landing on the runway, Rachel met the God like Los Antes mountain along the side view of the plane window that made her feeling God was just accompanying her by her side, the feeling was so special that showed the endless natural power and human's life was suddenly turning to be a piece of dust in the sky.........

It was kind of ancient Indian power accompanying the country's culture, she felt into wonderness at the moment. She booked a hotel room through the airport's stand and after that an airport bus took all the passengers heading to different hotels in the downtown of Santiago de Chile.

When she checked in Hotel La Plaza and settled down in a suite, it was already near 5:00 p.m. local Satiago time. She reminded the city view she just experienced was something very much like Buenos Aires but with more trees and less wide streets but mountain hills were around everywhere that made Satiago looking like a garden city with colorful trees and flowers, something romantic but also hidden behind somehow a kind of strong Indian and European mixed nature. It was a very beautiful city anyway......

Rachel connected through phone call with Mr. Peter Giowenka, the Cultural Attache of the Polish Embassy in Satiago; the lady secretary of Mr. Giowenka asked Rachel's room number and told her that she would ring her back in five minutes. After about eight minutes the lady called back saying, Mr. Ginwenka will visit her in the Hotel at 8 p.m.

Rachel relaxed then went to the bathroom to take a shower, after that she phoned the lobby counter to order a room service for some drinks at 8:10 p.m. in order to entertain the Cultural Attache.

It was still early for the appointed time, Rachel reviewed her file concerning the South Patagonia connections made by Hagen Duetch during the 50s. As soon as she finished that the door was knocked, it was still 7:30p.m., Rachel was suprised because it was early for the fixed time, she approached the door and found a tall guy in dark suit standing by the other side of the door through the door watching hole. "Who is it?" she asked in English. "A.N.I. agent, Miss Frida Cott." the person was naming her false name which is noted on the forged passport.

"Yes,..." Rachel opened the door. "Excuse me madam, it's a routine check. Please show me your passport." the guy was holding a wallet sized ID, written in dark blue letter 'ANI' "What does ANI mean, sir?" "Agencia National de Inteligencia, madam." the agent said. "Oh, shit, an agent again..." Rachel muttered then went back room to take the passport.

She returned to the doorside to show the agent the ID. The agent received the passport and slipped for a couple of pages then returned it immediately to Rachel saying: "It's a diplomatic passport, madam. welcome to Chile and sorry for bothering you." he quickly gave back the ID to Rachel. "Buenas noches!" the agent said and left. "Oh, again a police country." Rachel thought. She went back to her seat but didn't feel very confortable.

Five minutes late, the lobby counter called her saying, a gentleman is going to visit her and asking her permission to go to the suite. "Please send the gentleman up." Rachel said. "Yes, madam."

The door bell called, Rachel went to answer the door and met a Polish gentleman in very nice and elegant dressing; he is a thin and tall guy in his early fourties, thin mustache, white face and wearing thin gold flamed glasses. "Good evening, Miss Perlsztein, Peter Giowenka." "Oh, please come in. Mr. Cultural Attache."

Rachel invited Giowenka into the suite and both sitting on the living sofa. "How was your trip? Miss Perlsztein." "Everything was all right since it was not a very long hour trip." "Do you like Santiago?" "Yes, I viewed the scene while my way to here; it's a real beautiful City."

At this moment, the door bell was pressed, Rachel knew it was the room service guy so he asked an excuse and went to answer the door, the waiter followed her in with the cart and served the drinks then left."

Rachel began to serve the drinks and Giowenka helped her. It was Chilian style herb tea with cookies. Rachel tasted it but didn't like it very much but she didn't want to show any unpleasant feeling just saying: "It's a very nice and special taste tea." "Yes, it is. you know I have been get used with Chilian food and drinks." Giowenka said. "How long you have been working here, Mr. Giowenko?"

"Four years, my whole family is living here too." "Mr. Giowenka, I am going to visit south Patagonia on Chile's side within a couple of days; Do we have anybody there?" "Yes, I know where you want to go and I had phone our man there last night; We have an agent sited on that town whose name is Pan Brezeicri and I will give you his contact code; you could go there and to meet him directly; the contact is written on this small white card, you just keep it with care and tomorrow I will send him a secret call to advise him; You just go to meet him, anything you need he has to support you, okey?"

"Sure."

"Good. I suggest you to move to any hotel tomorrow before midday because ANI here is quite active." Giowenka said. "This evening, an agent of ANI had visited me." Rachel said. "Okey, it's normal. Anyway, you should take care in this country because they didn't change too much."

They went on talking for ten minutes then Giowenka quitted Rachel and left the hotel.

Rachel didn't feel very sure with this guy.

The next day afternoon Rachel left the Hotel and changed another samller one along the seaside and spent the same eveniing to sightseeing Satiago's beautiful night view. The second midday she departed from Santiago Airport to go to the southern Chilian City named Temuco, it was a close to coastal City about 500 kilometers south of Santiago. The flight took near one hour to reach the place; it was a so beautiful place when Rachel was forcusing the city's scene through her side window of the plane.

The airport was like any domestic airport of South American countries in a very Eurpoean and local mixed style.

She hired a cab to a downtown hotel tht allowed her to enjoy this southern fameous town's face.

There were narrow also wide ways among different part of the City; traditional Indian also modern flavor decorating with green parks and colourful trees; classic houses mixed local and European taste; quietness and peaceful city air; not too many tall buildings but houses across the city were colorful with art design, statures, squares and parks surrounding with bushes and trees; churches, watersprings, elegant cafes, shops. Latin American buildings, football staduims, bridges; it just like a piece of green jade located in the south of this narrow and long land......

The cab drove Rachel to a noble and elegant not very big hotel, the air around was as nice as the whole city; Rachel moved into the place with good mood, she even momently forgot Santiago..

When she began to take her afternoon cafe in her suite it was almost 5 p.m. local time.

After a room service dinner in the suite, he made a phone call to Mr. Pan Brezeicri, the Polish agent sited in Tomuco. "Hola,..." a middle aged man voice answered from the tube. "Mr. Brezeicri? This is Frida Cott calling." Rachel said. "Oh, Miss Cott, I received the call from Santiago, are you now here in Tomuco?"

"Yes. sir." Rachel said.

"I welcome you to my place tomorrow at 9:30 a.m. and I suppose you know the address, don't you? Please just take a cab, it's not far, I am living in the city, you can easily find it."

"Thank you, sir, I will be there on time."

"Okey." the phone then cut off.

The next morning was a sunny warm day.

Rachel left the Hotel about 9:15 a.m. then waved a cab by the doorway. Rachel showed the direction to the driver, the fat middle aged country guy nodded then started the engine heading to the destination. The morning's streets were quiet and clean also with less traffics, it took less than 10 minutes to get General Artigas 126, the Brezeecri's place.

Rachel paid the fare then got off. It was a smallsized house with a simple wooden gate coated in dark green paint, flowers and trees were behind the cement wall.

Rachel pressed the door bell and after a couple of minutes, a thin and literature weak like man in his middle fourties showed up by the door, he wore black thick flamed glasses, not too much hair, thick mustache too, he was looking really like a Chilian country guy. "Welcome to south Chile, Miss Perlsztein." the guy knew Rachel's true name. "Good morning, sir, it's so nice to meet you here." "Please come in." Pan invited Rachel in and began to lead the way to the living room.

They sat on the sofa of a not big living and Pan asked Rachel's permission then went to prepare two cups of Polish tea. "My wife and my daughter went to the neighbor town this early morning; we are three here." Pan said.

"I received the call from Santiago yesterday midday, they told me what you need; well, Miss Perlsztein, just tell me." Pan added.

"Are you also a historian working at Universidad de Tomuco, is that right."

"Yes, madam. I have been living in this town for 15 years."

"So, I just found a right person." Rachel said.

"We could exchange some points since I know you are a senior investagator of Warsaw U."

"Yes, I am."

"Okey, just shoot me." Pan said.

"What I need to know is that Hagen Deutch had been here once?"

"According to the record, yes, he did, but it was a long time ago, around 1951.."

"Did he come alone or with the couple?" Rachel asked.

"I am not sure the couple did come to this part of Patagonia, Los Antes is separating the both sides of Patagonia, you know." "What you mean is that the couple spent their life in the other side of Patagonia?"

"It's no more important they were or they weren't; I just would like reserve my opinion." "I understand that." Rachel said. "You know, sir. What I am interesting is that is any legancy still hidding in this side of Patagonia?" "I suppose no, if it had, only a very smallpart of it." "So, the main part is still hidding on the other side of Patagonia."

"Theorically yes, but maybe also hidding in some other places of Argentina, for example, Tucuman, Misiones, la Rioja, even Salta, anywhere could be..." Then, according to your investigation, Hagen knew everything before his death in 1967 in Virginia?" "Yes, he was the key person and he was more important then the couple." "What kind of leagancy that is still containing? gold? treasure? or some others materials?" "I can say that since I don't know either; it's a very confidential even sensible question, otherwise it should not be the main concern of so many countries inclunding the U.S., German, Raussia, Argentina, Isreal and also our homeland." Pan said. "Is Frank Kennedy the grandson of Hagen Duetch?" "Yes, We've got the DNA proof." "There is another saying that the 'Mine' is hidding in Canada also?" "I don't think so, because the distance was not allowed to do that."

Pan said. "So only Hagen Deutch knew the secret?" "And your late father." Pan said. "I don't know well my Dad's story since my mom also is dead." "I will tell you the story, young lady and that could be of helpful; but remember, it's a top secret, it was not important before, but right now; it's of great importance, you just listen and you should seal your mouth forever otherwise, if not only your own life but mine too." "Why do you trust me so much?"

"Because you are a key person of the case too." Pan said. "Do you suppose so many government don't know the secret?"

"Yes, they do. But they only know Frank Kennedy's part."

"Before I tell you the truth, you have got to answer me some questions?"

"Sure, sir."

"Okey, just tell me, are you Polish?"

"Yes, I am."

"Your father was a Polish?"

"Sure, he was."

"Was your Mom a Polish?"

"Sure, she was."

"Young lady, you still don't know very well of your own family."

Pan got up again to serve some other warm tea.

"Did I? What do you really mean?"

"Let me give you an account, then you would know it better; believe or not, but I just tell you as I know, okey."

"Okey, I will not be bothered by what you would tell me."

"Look, forgive me, first I have to mention your age; you were born in 1978 in Wasaw, right?"

"Yes, sir."

"Father Abraham Perlsztein, born in 1928 at a small Town near Wasaw of a Jewish family. Your late father was jailed in 1945 in Auschwitz Camp and met Hagen Duetch, he was then a SS Capitan in the camp and took your father as a young aide to supervise the inmates and that was the turn point of your late Dad's fate and he flee to Argentina with Hagen Deutch around 1946 through Spain or somewhere." Rachel just kept listening.

"The relationship between your late Dad and Hagen was very unclear; some investigators said they were a couple of lovers; and the great secret was that Hagen Deutch was a Jew himself but he was adopted by a German family after 1922, that was to say, when he was two years old. Between 1946 to 1963 your father had been working by Hagen's side in Argentina and he went on working as the assistant even the main key person for managing the couple and the Nazi group's financial affairs including the great treasure also some confidential Nazis's great secret under the couple's order during that period of time until the OLD MAN's death and the widow was little by little been driven out of the power circle. Your father flew with

Hagen to the U.S. through Miami in 1964 and three years later, Hagen died in Virginia. After Hagen's death, Abraham flew to Poonia in 1968 when he was 40 and in 1977 he married with your mother Rosa in Wasaw and the next year brought you to this world. Your Mom born in 1944 in Wasaw and she was also from a Jewish family. she died in 2000 in Wasaw when you were 22 years old. Okey, Miss Persztein, the rest story you knew it better than me; Please forgive me to tell you in such a straight way..." Brezcecri said.

"It's okey, sir. my mission is to find out the truth that happeded on this part of land and most importantly, to search the important staffs that nobody still has idea where those things are?"

"Okey, Miss Perlsztein, what I can help you is up to here. I could presnt you a person who is an Argentine historian now living in Puerto Monti, it's a port about 150 kilometers south from here; I can give you his address and you just go to visit him; of course, I will call him previously; His name is Ablerto Pieatti, but when you meet him, just call him 'Tio Pepe', okey."

"Omm..., Tio Pepe, I like the name." Rachel said. Then Brezcecri wrote down the address on a piece of peper:

Alberto Pieatti
Tio Pepe
Calle San Jose 247
Puerto Monti
Chile

He handled the paper to Rachel.

The lady quitted the house then took a cab back to the hotel.

The morning next Rachel checked out of the hotel haied a Remis with a driver to go to Puerto Monti. It was around 9:40 a.m., a bright sunny day. The driver drove the black car running along the beautiful and snaky coastal road heading to the south small sea port with maximum speed, it would take about one hour and ten minutes, the driver said. Chilian southern coastal road was a very fameous tourism route along the Pacific Oceon especially its blue greenish sea wave along the way.

The Remis arrived the port on time about 11 a.m. and the quiet sea port attracted Rachel immediately, colorful houses and trees, green moutain coverd by snow on the top, churches, small parts and lakes; boats and sails on the port side under the warm sunshine...; it just likes a paradise......

Rachel showed the driver the correct address and the middle aged guy asked a couple of passengers and just found the right street to reach San Jose 247. Rachel asked the driver to wait possibly a couple of hours or less to return back to Tomeco City; the driver just said she could take how much time she wnated. he parked the car then went to take coffee in the shop in front of the house.

Rachel pressed the door bell of the gate of a small residence by the street San Jose.

A tall and big well built guy came to answer the door, he was in his early fifties, semi gray haired, thick mustache, a pair of thick flamed glasses, semi white skinned also; he wore button down short sleeve blue shirt and a pair of white short pants. He met Rachel's eyes then studied a short while then smiled saying: "Are you Miss Perlsztein, welcome to Puerto Monti, yo soy Tio Pepe."

"Oh, Hello, Tio Pepe, I just coming from Temeco City."

"Come on in." Pepe opened widely the narrow gate. he led Rachel to go into his smallliving room. He invited Rachel to sit on the sofa and he went to the rear side and brought a 2 liters Coca Cola bottle with two glasses with ice cubics and served directly the Coke for both. Rachel didn't say anything.

"Pan called me last night and gave me the news of your visit; you know, I am living alone here, not for nothing, because this is a beautiful place for writing my books." Tio Pepe said. "Yes, Pan told me you are an Argentine historiasn." "Yes, I have been teaching in the UBA for near ten years and afterwards I began to do my researching works; I found this place a couple of years ago and I fell in love with her then I decided to stay here." Pepe said. "Look, Miss Perlsztein, I know why you are here, so just ask me anything you want and the midday, I invite you to eat in the food shop just in front of my house, they cook very well, you know; just like our Argentine saying, este es su casa, you know..." Pepe said. "Oh, Tio Pepe, you are too kind." Rachel said.

"That's okey, it's a long way for you to reach here."

"Thank you, sir, but would you also invite my driver to eat together?" Rachel said joking.

"Sure, what's the problem, I am not so poor in this smalltown." Tio Pepe laughed.

"Thank you, Tio, then I would like to ask you some questions."

"Just shoot me, senorita." Pepe said.

"How was the question of San Carlos, Bariloche?"

"It was the place los Nazis high ranking leaders lived after they arrived Cordoba after 1945."

"Was the couple also had been living in there?"

"You know who I mean?"

"Yes, they were, according my theory yes, but they were living a little far from San Carlos."

"How was the place?"

"It was a very huge mansion, so big that could allow more than fourty persons to live together; it was an very old house and so isolate only through boat and hydroplane one could reach that place." Pepe said.'But the couple had been lived in many different places in Argentina and they met a lot of their own people during such a long years and the house had a Radio device that could connect with Germany directly; Well, the couple had been many times in BA City too and they met with Juan D. too."

"How much value of gold and others treasures arrived to Argentina?" "Well, since 1941, they began to send gold to this country and that followed up to 1945, 1946...; the value at that time was too much over than 100 million U.S. dollars except thousands tons of extra values. but up to now the real value has been raising at lest mote than 100 billion U. S. dollars; we couldn't calculate it under the simple mathmathic addition but through economic influence, since you know, the German and Vantican bankers in Argentina used to control and developing their domains on the country's fate; well, you are a wise young lady, you should quickly catch the sanse, yes..."

"I see."

As the rumors followed along the years, people said some bishops and monsignors were involoving in the continuous conspiracy, is that right?" Rachel added. "I don't want to mention their names." Tio Pepe admitted.

"During 1946 up to 1948, tons of Nazis came to Argentina under Red Cross passport and they carried the great value into the country too."

"It's an openly secret, John D. and his wife did it through an European small country." Pepe said.

There was a historical name as Bormann's Treasure', how was that?" "Well, that money came into Argentina through air and sea way since 1941 or 1942 and I don't want to detail it."

"Well, Tio Pepe, do you know the name Hagen Deutch?"

"Yes, he died in 1967 in Virginia at 60."

"Was he a SS Major General?"

"No, he was only a SS Capitan before 1945 in Polish concentration camp."

"Is Frank Kennedey his grandson?"

"Yes, he is. The surname Kennedy was forged when he arrived Miami Migerations under an Irish Passport written Hans Kennedy."

"How did he forge an Irish passport?"

"He didn't forge it but bought it by an amount of money since you know during that old time everything could be forged; let's forget Europe, in Argentina one could do anything with money and let's just put him as a common guy not a Nazis criminal, yes..."

"Sure, Professor." Rachel said.

"Well, young lady, what are you really looking for?"

"I can't tell you sir, but I appreciate your information."

"There are tons of secrets arounfd the topics, you would never learn them all."

"What I need is to get some key confidential points that would be enough for my work."

"I am just a historian but I would like to tell you what I had learnt."

"Then I would ask you some very sensitive questions?"

"Sure, senorita, Vd, puede perguntarme como quieres." Pepe said.

"Do you believe in your government?"

"No, absolutely not."

"Why are you living in this foreign country but not far from your homeland?"

"But this country is acturally a pro-Nazis idea country too."

"Yes, it is, but Chile and Argentina used to be enemy to each other for a long time."

"So, you are living in a safe place?"

"Not exactly, but anyway, one should find a place to stay." Pepe said.

"Do you think La Falta, San Carlos, San Miquel de Tucuman are all possible places to hide Nazis treasure?"

"I am not sure the treasure is still hidding in some place or it had already turned to be Argentine currency after so long years..."

"Why?"

"Because Argentina used to be a shadow powered government through generation after generation."

"Why so many South American historians even European history researchers are still working so hard for the question?"

"Because nobody is holding 100% evidence." Pepe said.

"Young lady, let me first invite you for a simple lunch in front my house and afterwords let's go on chatting, okey."

"Okey, but as I told you an hour ago, let my Remis driver to have lunch with us too and be my guest."

"Look I only invite you to eat fameous Argentine food, Minanesa de Pollo con Papa Frita and vivo blanco, you would like it."

"What's that?"

"Fried Argentine chicken with French chips and White wine.".

"That sounds delicious!"

"Well, then let's go.' Pepe smiled.

Pepe led Rachel to cross the street and arrived the food shop named 'Hermoso Monti'. They chose a table on the other side of the shop window just focusing the far view of the blue colored sea port, it looked just like a real painting.

The young waiter seemed like knowing Pepe very much, he neared Tio Pepe with a gentle smile. "Por favor traiame dos porciones de minanesas de pollos con papa fritas y medio de vino blanco y tambien invitarme el chaufer de Remis que venga aca para comer junto con nosotros." said Pepe.

"Como no, jefe, en serquita." the mozo answered then withdrowed. He first went to the counter to make the order then went personally to outside to ask the driver to come in to have lunch with Pepe.

The driver came in with a smile but he insisted to sit far from the table of Pepe and Rachel since he didn't want to bother them.

The order was served after about 15 minutes and Rachel and Pepe went on chatting but nobody heard anything.

At this monent, a patro car stopped by the shop and two soldier like guys in gray uniform came into the shop, first they went to talk with the bartender then coming near the table of Pepe saying: "Buenos tardes, senor. Somos agentes de ANI, podria decirme quien es esta mujer?"

"Oh, ella es una pariente que venca de Buenos Aires para visitarme y ya va volver por la misma tarde." Pepe said. "Podemos ver el passporte de ella?"

"Como no." Pepe answered then muttered to Raquel to show her ID. in English. "Rachel didn't feel very glad but she did it. One of the soldiers took the passport then through his scanner on the cover of Rachel's passport, the merchine made a bi noise. "Muy bien, que tenga Vds muy buenas tardes." then they went out of the shop.

"What's a fucking police country is this?" Rachel felt very unconfortable. Well, Miss Perlsztein, we are in South America, besides, they are a couple of local police dogs." Pepe said.

"They said they are of ANI." Rachel said.

"Yes, they just said that, but they are not really belonging to ANI but a pair of assholes they are runing for ANI to catch information." "You have to get used to them while you are staying on South America land. the SIDE Argentina is the same but they sometimes would do it more skillfully, but they are of the same kind of shit."

"You know, my passport is a diplomatic one." Rachel said.

"In this small town, some police even wouldn't read well." Pepe said.

"They don't know you since you have been living in here for several years?"

"Yes, maybe, but they only know money, besides they don't like Argentine people."

"Sorry for the disruption, please Miss Perlsztein, just enjoy the food." Rachel began to eat little by little and after a while she got relaxed with a little bit of wine.

They went back to Pepe's home was around 1 p.m., Rachel decided to speak with Pepe one more hour in oder to catch a little more information.

Pepe went to the kitchen prepared a pot of Te Misiones with lemon and sugar then brought it onto the table and went on talking with Rachel.

"It was true that German had sold to Japan near the end of the war about hundres of kilograms of Urianium Oxide to Japan in order to change tons of cash?" "I don't want to comment that because FBI knew it better." "Did FBI spent a lot time to investigate many case of Nazis in Argentina?"

"Yes, they did, but there was no any report to be published."

"Did the U.S. knew anything about the important Treasure's whereabouts?"

"It has been a decades long continuous follow-up and the case is open and ongoing." Pepe began to lit his cagar.

"Do you seggest me to visit some more places in Argentina?"

"I suppose so if you really want to dig something out, but I couldn't garentee you that you could find something at the end.'

"While did you say so?"

"Because it will be too dangerous for you if you will be alone and on yourself."

"Thank you sir. I understand that."

"Tio Pepe, as I know, you have got several books published, all you had told was true?" "Maybe 80% of that was true but the rest 20% is for attracting some other authors to say by themselve and little by little, the truth will be coming out." Pepe said.

"As I know, you Argentine are Jantas that means you Argentines are not too honest and you guys used to lie." "I will not say no, lady. but sometimes, we could do anything straightly without too many tricks..., it's our character, only Argentine could against Argentine, you know."

"Well, Miss Perlsztein, beware when you are leaving Chile and I suggest you to go back to Europe first and after that, you could come back to South America to Argentina because Argentine SIDE is very advanced in its technology, they have nothing less than CIA, you know." Pepe said. "Are you not a SIDE agent, Tio Pepe, aren't you." "I don't know, you have to judge me." Pepe smiled.

Rachel discussed with Tip Pepe for half hours more then she decided to go back to Tomeco City by the same ramis cab.

She appreciated Tio Pepe the began to take the same way back along the coastal road. it was 3:30 p.m. She would be back to Tomeco at around 5 p.m.

Along the road back to Tomeco City, Rachel was falling in a very deep thoughts; she found a piece of half page of photocopiied old yellowish paper written on a kind of ancient ink as the following and she knew it well that that piece of the paper was only the last part of the whole page and where is the rest page of the paper? "It is in Frank Kennedy's hand." Rachel said to herself.

Tres anos despus Sal V. S Peter Km 110 S-27 km w/cross SWALISKA-UP derecho Simbro-santa-cross de la sierra Miss Perlsztein couldn't understand nothing on the paper; she kept the original one in her Wasaw's home; it's of the great importance.

Rachel couldn't find any clue on the paper either. The remis cab returned to the Hotel at almost 5 p.m. the local time.

She went to upstairs room and took a shower first; after that he made a phone call directly to her Embassy sited in Buenos Aires; she applied to speak to his excellence the Ambassdor Mr. Polonsky.

The Embassy answered her phone directly by his desk. "Yes, Miss Perlsztein, do you have any news for me?" "No, sir, I am waiting for your further indication." "Okey, you may first go back hometown to check the the details about Hagen Deutch and take a trip to Berlin to confirm it and after that you will still have time to go back to BA City and trying to get connection with Franky Kennedy there, as I just have noticed that, the U.S. was just leaving Miami heading to Rio and the next week they will be arriving BA City; of course, we will update you in every step, okey." "Yes sir, I understand"

"Good luck and have a nice trip."'

Chapter twenty

Rachel booked through the Hotel counter an air ticket to go back to Wasaw via Amsterdam from Lan Chile Airlines night service for the next morning 11:00 a.m.

She checked out from the Hotel at nine o'cock then hired a cab to go to Temuco Airport; the morning flight had not many passengers especially from this small southern Chilan town; the plane first reached Santiago for a short stop then heading directly to Amsterdam, there was only a coffee service before arriving Satiago.

Lan Chile 263 landed on Satiago to take more passengers for going to Europe; Only a couple of minutes before taking off, the air attendent was going to close the plane door, two dark suit coated young guys slipped in and heading directly to Rachel's chair. One of the agents saying:" Excuse me miss, may I see your ticket and passport please? We are ANI agents." the guy said so while showing her a small wallet sized ID. "Why not." Rachel took out her ID and ticket from her perse to give to the guy.

They both studied the papers for a while and exchanged a few words in Spanish then said:" Thank you miss, everything is in order." then they left the plane. "All the agents around the world are the same, no brains but to bother people." Rachel felt somehow very unplansant feeling at the moment.

The plane taxied itself to the runway and ready to taking off. "Oh, at least I am going home." Recher said to herself.

After a little more than four hours the flight arrived San Pablo and started a non-stop trip to go to Amusterdam, it should take another ten hours. Rachel asked the stewardess a sleeping pill for being a long hours rest. When she work up it only needed near two hours to get Amsterdam.

When she returned to Wasaw City it was around midday local time. She went back to her flat for a long hours sleep, it was next morning 8 a.m., a claudy and raining morning, she made a phone call to AGENCIA WYWIADU (Polish Foreign Intelligence Agency) for an appointment and the chief of international operation gave her a space for 3 p.m. the same afternoon.

Rachel presented in the office and reported a summary of her Pam-American tour concerning the project.

"After such a long years, everything has been getting so unclear and confused; any international trails or low suit one against the other would not get any final result because the old time is dead and the Nazis power and robbed treasure had already meling into every corner of the greastest power of the world; but one thing we still can do is to find Hagen Deutch's treasure in Patagonia or somewhere else who knows; What we want is to give a little return for the generations of the former Holocost victims who lost both their lives and money; thousands tons of gold had been lost; What is still hidding under Hagen Deutch's project was and still is the small part of treasure we could hunt it out, of course a lot of other kinds of top secrets and information even materials and technology are mined together with that, therefor the U.S. and German even the local Argentine governments are all forcusing on this aim; but Rachel, your mission is just to pressure Frank Kennedy to solve the secret and find whereabouts of the things we are finding, then your goal will be completed, that's the main point; Now that you should go to Berlin to check details about Hagen's true Jewish name through its National Achives and go back to the U.S. trying to get the other part of the paper then you could go down to South America to follow up Frank Kennedy, of course all our agencies everywhere will back up you at any moment, you won't worry about that? Is that clear." the chief Mr. Rondonsoviwicz said.

"Very clear sir." Rachel answered.

"Then when you are going to Berlin?"

"In a couple of days."

"Good luck." the chief got up and gave Rachel his hand.

Rachel stayed in Warsaw for a couple of days and especially she went to the Jewish cementary to visit her parents' graves; they were two graves located in different places of Warsaw suburban since her Dad was buried with his first wife and Rachel's mother married her Dady when he was a widower after his first wife died in illness; the God's fate made them met and married but they both didn't have long life; Rachel's Dad died in heart attack in his sixties and her Mom also died in heart illness several years after therefore she lost them in a very young age and after that her life was hard and tough; Rachel heritaged her mother's appearence, blonde and very pure white skinned also her strong character.

Everytime when Rachel went to see her mother with flowers, she used to miss the road around so many Jewish tombs, but there was a path guide was that Mr.Buyer's tomb was standing at the head of the channel where her mother's tomb was; so whenever she met Mr.Buyer's smiling picture on his tomb plane she knew where was the right position to turn left in and walking for a couple of meters she could find her mom's place easily.; whenever Rachel met Buyer;s face she used to put her finger to give Buyer a hand kiss to appreciate his direction; life is turning as a circle also running as a dream but the sense is always with endless sadness.

Rachel put one of her knee in front of her tumb then put the flowers into the vase, she said many words to her beloved mother and cried....

She used to wish oneday she could bury just on her mother as Jewish tradition did; but sometimes God's will couldn't always fix person's wish.

She left the cementry after about 30 minutes prayer and left the place before washing her hands along the way out of the cementary; it was a Jewish tradition.

Rachel used to miss her Dad very much but there was something that always stopped her to visit her Dad, she didn't know really why, but it was the life....

Rachel went on staying in Wasaw one more day and on the fourth day, he took a short flight to go to Berlin; she needed to visit Bundesarchiv Office in the City.

Hagen Deutch's original Jewish name should be confirmed.

Berlin, Germany, April 2012

It was a warm and sunny pleasant morning when Rachel arrived the City of Berlin.

She has been in Berlin many times and this time she arrived to this classic and modern mixed place let her to review every beautiful things around the city again; she easily found the Office and met a middle aged lady working on the second floor in charge of secret criminal information affairs. Rachel neared her desk and greeted her in German first: "Guten tag! Ich bin Rachel Perlsztein, Ish komme aus Poland und..." she explained what she wanted.

"Good morning, my name is Anna Anderson, would you first fill out this form for the information you want and please put your reason of your inquiry nature." the German woman didn't like Rachel's German and responded her in a very strong Berlin accented English while she drew out a sheet of white form and pushing to the side where Rachel was sitting. Her attitute was with a very German pride..

"Sure, miss. I will do it right now." Rachel said. "Okey, please go to the side table to do it and when you will finish it just turn me back then you need to wait the answer for at least three business day if our office would grant your application." the woman called herself Anderson said without any expression.

"Madam, I am here under the name of Polish Foreign Ministry to beg you to do that." Rachel showed her a white name card written her name together with the logo of PFM."

The woman peeked the card then took off her desk phone and intending to speak with someone in German language. After a couple of minutes, Anderson got up saying,

"Would you follow me to the upstairs?" she took the form too. The woman led Rachel to go the upstair through an classic staircase and arriving an office, she pushed the door open then invited Rachel to go in to sit.

"Plese just wait, our chief will be with you in a minute." Ana Anderson said then left.

It was an ancient style very noble like room, dark red carpet, a classic long conference table with many chairs around; Rachel chose a side chair to sit herself down.

The two twin long windows on the orher side of the wall one could forcus on the Berlin's City view.

A tall and elegant German gentleman in his middle thirties coated in dark brown suit showed up with a mere gentle smile. "Good morning, Miss Perlsztein, is that correct?" "Yes, sir." Rachel said.

"I just checked the question you inquired through our electronic record and we couldn't find any name matched it and I am sorry that we can't give you any information; According to your application form, the man on the paper was a deseased man and he was an U.S. citizen; so I suggest you to find the information you need through the U.S. State Department or any U.S. Embassy around." the guy said.

"But he was a German citizen." Rachel said.

"Yes, he was, but it was a long time ago and he left Germany after 1945."

"You just said, he left this country after 1945?"

"Because your paper declared this information.' the man said.

"I am sorry, Miss Perlsztein, we can't help you but before you go please make a signature on this paper otherwise we couldn't finish the process."

The man put the same form on the table just infront of Rachel.

"May I have other choice?"

"No, you may not, madam."

Rachel did it and left the office with disappointment, but she knew that the German authority didn't want to give any information about Hagen Deutch because they knew the man quite well and it was a delicate case.

Rachel decided to leave the country as soon as she could in order to avoid any dangerous incident to be happened.

She just realized that diplomatic concern sometimes was very powerful but also powerless in case the multipower is involved.

Every pare is a chess player.

She took the afternoon flight rushly back to Wasaw hometown. Rachel went back to her flat and found her place was under searching during her absence.

The second day was just on Saturday, she drove to Warsaw U. campus with idea to stay in the Libary to think over what allabouts in order to take next step.

She prtked her dark blue small VW outside the Library then took the long steps to reach the gate; she went to the second floor through a birdcage copper elevator and chose a seat to sit herself down in a big and tall hall.

She figured out that Frank Kennedy's group would arrive Buenos Aires in a couple of days and according to her, the team would not get anything new after a round trip through Argentina; at least she supposed that they wouldn't find any treasure but the points were that sometimes, the multi-gobernmental group doesn't have idea to find treasure but something too much important than money; "The group will be back with an empty hnad." Rachel thought.

"But the government of Poland only wants to hunt Hagen Deutch's hidding treasure but there still has not any clue to show any sign of the correct place." "Polish government suggests that the goods is hidding in soewhere of Argentina but anyway, who really knows?" Rachel thought.

"This was an old account between Nazis criminals and Holocaust victims and it's also a current general concern for many countries which had involoving the question during the World War II and it also is an old personal account between her Dad and Hagen Deutch and as an Polish Federal Agent she would have no choice." Rachel thought.

At this moment an middle aged Polish gentleman in his middle fifties neared the table where sitting Rachel saying:" Would you mind I sit infront of you, madam?" the guy wore middle season dark suit, white shirt and dark brown tie, he had a thin long but soft face.

"Of course no, sir. please take your seat." Rachel said.

"Thank you." the guy pulled out the chair then sat himself down.

"My name is Joseph Shoemann, I am a vice-professor of this Faculty; I am teaching human science..." Shoemann presented himself.

"Oh, It's very nice to meet you here."

"Thank you, Miss Perlsztein."

"Do you know me?" Rachel said with somehow a little suprise.

"I know you and also your Dad." Shoemann said slowly.

"You mean, you knew my Dady Abraham Persztein?"

"Yes, I did."

"Then, you should know Hegan Deutch also?"

"Not exactly, but I heard his name from Arraham."

"Then you knew something my Dad and Hagen Deutch?"

"You can say that again."

"Can you tell me something about the secret between my Dad and Hagen Deutch?"

"They had been very very close partners since the year they met at the first time in the concentration camp and after that along the years they spent in Argentina after 1945 even they went together to the U.S. and after Hagen's death in 1963, your Dad went back to his homeland and met your Mom Rosa in 1977 and the second year you were born; your Dady never was a poor guy but his great regretness was that he didn't own the treasure which was the great secret he shared with Hagen during the time they spent in Argentina; because after Hagen's death, he only held the part of that page and the other part of the page was keeping in Hagen's hand until his death; Dr. Frank Kennedy even his Dad, I mean Steven Kennedy both didn't know anything about the treasure; during so long time world investigations, several G countries knew that someting of great importance concerning that treasure mine which including some top confidential Hi-Tech even UFO's most advanced technologies that Third Reich had obatained long time before the U.S. and Rassian; so the most intensive concern of G-countries is not for the old money but the hidden technologies; But miss Perlsztein, for my old time sake with your late father I suggest you to get away from the question although your homeland wishes you to discover the case, but listen to me, it's a great dangeous thing if you begin to touch any discovery of that; Do you know what I mean?" Shoemann said.

"Yes, I understand."

"But how can I believe in you?" Rachel added.

"I don't want your trust because I am completely out of the case; Since I knew your late parents and as I know your grandparents were also the victims of the concentration camp; only for this reason, you should only to find some personal treasure from the mine but not any other things that so many governments are concerning; You are a wise girl, you would know how to manage the situation." Shoemann said peacefully.

"What you meant is that I only need to show my work indirectly."

"Exactly, in one simple word, you only need to find your personal treasure with Frank Kennedy undercoverly; other things just let the G- countries to solve by themselves; the War II has been over for more than 67 years, it's no more worth to find any ruins of that."

"Why my Dad kept so long time tight relationship with Hagen?"

"Because, if you don't mind, they had been a long time gay lovers since they both were bi-sexual in life."

"Ommmu..., now I understand." Rachel said.

"Do you still hold that half page of old paper?" Shoemann asked.

"I can't tell you."

"Try to get another part of the page from Franky, but the original one; because the government is holding him to go to South America with a piece of false paper; So Franky's life will be depending on the resault of the finding, you know?"

"What you mean is I have to save Franky's life?"

"You just catch the point."

"But how could I achieve that?"

"Do you remember Issac Schtok?"

"Yes, but he is an officaial agent of Israel government.'

"Yes, he is and he is also the agent of MOSSAD."

"What's hell Issac Schtok to do with me?"

"Yes, he would help you to achieve your goal because he knew your late mother."

"He is not too much older than me, only eight years."

"That's nothing to do with the age; you have to see Issac as a friend not a 100% agent.'

"Mr. Shoemann, are you an Israel agent too.'

"No, I am not, lady; but don't forget one thing, we are all Jews."

"Is Franky Kennedy a Jew?"

"Yes, he is."

"And Hagen Deutch too, but he betraied his homeland also himself. he was a Nazis criminal.'

"Okey, I have to go, Good luck, Miss Perlsztein." Shoemann got up from his chair.

"Where could I find you later?"

"In here, University of Wasaw if I would still alive." Shoemann smiled then left.

Chapter twtenty one

Buenos Aires, Aprol 2012

James Smith led one term of investigation for the case arrived Buenos Aires from Virginia through Miami. Kauffmann, Issac Schtok, Frank Kennedy were of the three key members; besides they would cooperate with the local U.S. special agents of FBI and CIA in order to start the innitial research for the plan. Before doing anything, they decided to make a meeting which was taking in the U.S. Embassy located in the area of Plaza Italia of the BA City. Since the day of their arriving, Rachel had received the first hand information through the Foreign Ministry of Poland then she took the first plane to go back to Buenos Aires, this time she used the secind firged Polish Passport under the name of Henlla Linkivsky, her profession was a natural plant investigator of the National Institute of Biology. she cut the hair and changed the look but still an elegant pretty young lady. It was only a couple of days after Smith's group arriving.

Miss Henlla Linkivsky was received in Enzeza International Aurport by Polish Consul in Buenos Aires, he helped her to passed the Migeration process rapidly then took her by his car to settle down in a nice flat located in Recoleta area in the middle part of the City.

As soon as Rachel left the airport, the SIDE Argentina had identified that Rachel Perlsztein and Henlla Linkivsky were the same person. They just put the data into the computer for following up. The next morning was on Saturday, a sunny warm pretty air around the garden like neighborhood mixed with noble gentle classic and modrn buildings and houses; Buenos Aires used to be a multicultural metropolytain, different zone of the City representing somehow specail European regional native flavors, it was somthing romantic over this south soil.

She stoped by a payphone along the sidewalk she was walking and made a call to the number she noted on her smallnotbook.

"The line got through, 'Hola...'" an eldly very low but clean voice answered.

"Hola, puedo hablar con el senor Jacobo Glossman?"

"Si, Vd estar con el, de parte de quine?" the old man answered.

"Buenos dias, senor Glassman, yo soy Raquel, vivo de Polonia. puedo ir a su lugar?"

"Oh, bien viendo a la ciudad, por supuesto Vd. puede vinir aca; el direccion es Avenida Colonel Diaz 1978, Piso sexto."

"Ha.., gracias senor, me voy ahora."

"Te espero a las 10:30 a.m." the old guy cut the line. It was not so far the address from the place she was calling, but Rachel stopped a cab to go to the house. it was around 10:20 a.m.

The weekend morning was clean and fresh also having not much passengers and traffic on the streets.

Colonel Diaz Avenue was a residential not very wide street cross the fameous Santa Fe 3400 more or less. It took only more than a couple of minutes to get the place and arriving an elegant building.

She paid the fare after getting off and just met a middle aged doorman standing on the sidewalk of the building, Rachel showed him the number on her notebook.

"Oh..., senor Glassman estar en 6A, adelante por favor, senorita." The doorman raised a morning smile and showed the entrnce for Rachel with his index finger; he was still smoking his morning cigarette.

Rachel followed one of the two lines elevator and quickly arrived the six floor.

An old man in his middle seventies already standing by his door to receiving Rachel since the doorman had advised him through the secret intercom for the lady's visiting.

"Buenos dias, senorita Raquel, soy Jocobo Glassman, muchos gustos de conocela" Jacobo gave his hand to Rachel.

Rachel could see a series light green faded number on the front part of his right arm that evidently meant he was in Nazis concentration camp during the War II period.

Jacob invited Rachel to go into his modern and confortable living, a big full sized glass door on the other side of the wall connecting directly to the balcony which was facing onto the quiet street downstaris.

As soon as Rachel sat on the long sofa, an elderly woman who had more or less the similiar age of Jacobo showing up, then the old man introduced her as his wife Berlta; the woman had a sharp point nose, heavy make-up, very commercial like... Berlta sat by Jacoba shoulder by shoulder then their conversations got started.

"Senor Jacobo, since you were foreign Polish citizen, I need your help to identify a person, well, he is no more in this world; but as we know, you had a year long was holding in the concentrationg camp before 1945 in Auschwitz, could you remember this person...?" Rachel said while showing the picture of Hagen Deutch in his SS black Nazis uniform. Jacobo peeked on the picture just saying, "Of course, I remember this son of bitch; he was Capitan Hagen Deutch."

"Could you remember his nick name?"

"We all called him 'Devil', he was worse than a devil."

"And do you remember a guy then more or less as your age, his name was Abraham Persztein?"

"He was Hagen's gay lover; Hagen gave him a rank as Sergeant and he was the close asistant by Hagen, but I never have seen him again after the war."

"Why could you remember Abraham so well?" Rachel asked.

"Because once he and me were on Hagen's bed together."

"You mean,...., Hagen had also had relation with you?"

"Yes, but because he liked any boy as my age in the camp therefore once I was chosen and he raped me."

"Only once?"

"Yes, once was enough. he ruined my life."

"You know, senor Jacobo, Abraham Persztein was my Dad."

"Oh, sorry, I didn't know that..."

"No problem, I didn't know that neither." Rachel said. Jacobo's wife didn't say anything just sitting by her husband.

"How did you escape from the death camp?"

"Well, as one of the Hagen's favorite boys. I ran back through Rex Cross frist to Swissland, of course after a lot of difficulties and on there I obtained an Argentine passport under my fake Nazis ID, it was an ID I stole ftrom a dead Nazis soldier and with that ID more than 1,500 U.S. dollars I could buy an Argentine passport therough theri offical agent in Swissland; well, you sure will ask me how could I get such a lot of cash, it was a question besides..."

"I could understand that." Rachel said.

"What I need is to discover Hagen's real nick name."

"Well, I couldn't help you Miss Perlsztein and I hope you will get it through others sources."

"What do you mean?"

"Yes, go to AMIA, maybe they could help you." Jacobo said.

"Where is the AMIA?"

"Ask any cab driver could easily find it, it's close to the corner of Tucuman 2300 and Pasteiur."

"Thank you so much, senor Jacobo Glossman." Rachel said. The couple accompanied Rachel up to the flat door.

Rachel came out of Jacobo's building then found a payphone along the block to call Polish Embassy. She gave her code number to the phone receptionist as soon as the line got through and she was attended immediately by an officer at the other end of the line. "Good morning, Miss Persztein, my name is Marko Polansky, the special agent of the Embassy, how can I help you?" "Yes, I need to go to AMIA for some information." "No, you should not, because they have MOSSAD agent sited there, it's against the rule,"

"Really...?"

"Yes, the better way is to go any shop in the Jewish Town in ONCE area and you would have better lucky and easily to get what you want, but anyway be careful; You know how to arrange, don't you."

"Thank you for the suggestion, Mr. Polansky, I will try."

"Okey, good, anytime." the line was cut.

Rachel took a Taxi to go to ONCE, the black and yellow coated can spent about ten minutes to reach the spot she wanted, it was around Corrientes 2200 and Jose E. Uriburu 400; she paid the fare then got off the semi old oil can.

The place was just in the middle central part of Jewish Once Town, mostly hundreds of wholesale shops from A to Z were concentrating in that ten by eight blocks commercial area; among them some Jewish religionousl schools and Sinacorques were located there two; there mixed Azshinazi Jewish also Sefalatin Jewish folks besides some traditional Kosha butchers shops and barkeries even bookstores, jewlery house, old clock house and Jewish food restaurants and free food joint for poor people; In Argentina Jewish guys had nick name as Moisenles or Los Rusos just liked Arabia people was called as Tuco and Italian was called as Tano and Spaniard as Gallego and Chinese as Fu-Man-Chu or Chin-Chu-Lin and in reality, Chi-Chu-Lin was a kind of local Argentine food made by cow's indestines....

After 1996 a lot of Chinese guys from Chinese mainland came to Buenos Aires to run mini-supermarkets or the whole sale for- "All One Dollar" shops as well as Koreans were monopolying ready made clothes in cheap prices that effected great much Jewish traditional self-run markets....

But Jews used to control financial power in everywhere, so small merchants from others countries only could insult Jews as "Rusos de la Mieta" (Fucky Jewish Shit) caused by envy.

A Jewish leather shop attracted Rachel's attention, it was an old leather goods store located not many steps from the corner of Jose E. Uriburu 400 and some old staff leather coats were displaying next to the shopping window with very cheap prices.

Rachel liked a fur hat also a good quality lady's leather made money clip; then she stepped into the shop.

Buenas tardes, sonorita,,,; Busmandeje,,, Flau...?" an elderly woman greeting her in both language and the second one seemed like Yiddish or something. "Buenas tardes...!" Rachel answered with a gentle smile.

The sales lady neared Rachel began to attend in full Yiddish, she seemed had noticed that the European young lady was of Jewish community.

Rachel couldn't speak very perfectly Yiddish but she had learnd something from her late Mom Frida when she was a little and she also could speak quite well Russian idiom which was taught by her Dad Issac Perlsztein who was a Russain Medical Doctor during his lifetime.

She chose a couple of articles then paid in U.S. dollars cash, the shop owner was happy to get such a quick buyer.

After that, Rachel showed her the old picture and asked the old woman if she knew that guy? "Everybody in that camp knew him and hated him." the old woman said in Yiddish, she was looking as old as 75.

"Of course, when i was still a very pretty teens." she said with a Jewish-like smile.

"Could you remember his nick name?" Rachel asked. "Everybody called his as 'Devil'..." the woman said.

"I mean, the the real nick name or purposely his real middle name or first name?"

"Just let me think..." while the woman put the green cash into the copper made register merchine

The old but fine antique made a claer 'Ding..!" noise.

"Yes, now I remember,... it's DAVID.'". that's right; his Jewish name is David."

"Are you sure?" Rachel said.

"Yes, sure, sure, that son of thousand bitches was called as David too; because...., you know why, once Ericmann came and called him 'David'..., and something more liked David Socovitch... something like dthat."

"Oh..., David Socovitch." Rachel amde a deep breath but she intended for not showing any suprise... "Gut, madam." Rachel said then continued, "Please give me half a dozon more the same kind leather clips, I need to make some presents to my friends in my return." Rachel said while she began to draw some green notes out of her wallet. "Sure, madam." the old woman's gray green Jewish eyes began to shine as the same green color of the U.S. green back.

"Are you Arthkinazc?" Rachel asked the woman.

"No, I am Sefanatin of Spain." the woman smlled, "But you are an Arthkinazc."

"Yes, I am." Rachel answered.

"You are a very pretty young lady."

"Thank you. But as I know Sefanatin women are very hot also beautiful."

"You can say that again, I am still very hot; You know why? because my husband is a Tuco butcher and he used to close his

Kushak shop nearby and coming back to make love with me along the business hour." Rachel listened just made a gentle smile then quit the shop heading to downtown with a cab.

"I am looking for it around the world but I naver image the secret discovered so easily and suprisely." Rachel though on the ride.

Just getting off the Taxi, Rachel's cellphone vibrated.

"Hello...?"

"Miss Perlsztein. This is Warco Darkensien speaking, the special agent of Polish Embassy in BA City. Please meet me at 3 p.m. at Mozat Music Cafe in Florida 565 and I have got a very important indication to tell you personally; Don't worry, I know you through our file; Listen carefully, after we will meet, then we would decide to change place to talk because the cellphone used to be tapped, yes."

"Yes sir." Rachel answered then cut the line.

It was around 2:20 p.m., she still got time for a quick lunch.

Chapter twenty two

Florida 565 is a quiet classic French style coffee shop located on BA's most luxious tourist fasion street; you could call it as Paris, London or New York as you like and in reality it used to be a beautiful flavor street combining a mixed European culture; but right now, in the year 2012, it has been actually faded with the time but one could still feel somehow a piece of old time shadow.

Rachel arrived on time at 3 p.m. Someone was sitting in the rear side of the Cafe made her a hand sign; a middle sized gentleman in his early fourity dressing in middle season drak gray suit, half beard head, a pair of dark blue sunglasses; he was white skinned typical East European guy.

Rachel noticed the man then heading directly to his table, the gentleman got up previously to wait for the lady's arriving.

"Good afternoon, Miss Perlsztein. Warco Darkensien." "It's so nice to meet you, sir." Rachel answered in Polish. "Please sit down." "Thank you, sir."

Rachel and Darkentein sat face to face by a small round table near the wall; an eldly male waiter came to take order

gently and silently. "Cafe Holanda." Rachel said. "Make it two."
Warco said to the waiter with a gentle and high class smile.

"Look, Miss Perlsztein. This is the address we have to meet
again about half an hour later; it's not very far from here, you
would call a cab to get there; you know, eyes are everywhere..."
Warco pushed a paper slip to Rachel on the table. "I see, sir."
Rachel took the slip then pushed it into her purse.

The waiter arrived again and served two small cups of
coffee then left.

Warco finished the coffee quickly then took the bill heading
to the counter in the front. "I have got to go first, lady; you may
leave ten minutes later." he said to Rachel before his leaving.

"No problem, sir."

Rachel left the shop a while later and began to window-
shopping the street while she opened the paper slip to read the
written addtess:

Cafe Garden Viejo
El Puente Viejo, La Boca

As soon as she walked up to the corner of Cordoba Avenue,
she waved a cab to go to the written address. It took avoult ten
more minutes to reach the old La Boca sea port; She noticed the
old iron made fameous old La Boca bridge standing over the
dirty river which was connecting the BA City and its cross river
neighbor town Avellaneda, a industrious spot next to Lanus,
another town closed to Avellaneda.

La Boca still maintaining several old whorehouses in their
original colorful paint as a tourist attractive sign.

Dozons of tango type cafes and theaters and antique shops were gathering around; the real business hours and showtime used to take place after sunset.

Rachel easily found the Cafe Garden Viejo, she steppped into the shop, an old tangquero bartender was cleaning his counter by himself; only a couple of worker like guys were taking coffee by the traditional kind of old wooden table by the window on the other side........

"Buenas tardes, senorita Perlsztein, pasa por aca por favor...!" the bartender greeted Rachel and showed a table not far from the door to her; Rachel got great suprise was that why the guy had already knew her surname. "Gracias, senor." Rachel didn't say anything then took the seat by the table.

A cup of traditional La Boca Tango cafe was served immediately on the table; the bartender winked his eye and showing a gentle smile then went back to his place.

A kind of slow tango music song was floating in the air...

About a couple of minutes later, Warco came into the cafe and heading directly to Rachel's table.

He sat down and began to converse with Rachel, the bartender neared him to serve a cup of expresso cafe. The wooden table hwere thay were sitting had no tablecloth, only a CINZANO metal made ashtray; the surface of the table had a lot of different names and dates marked or written with black marker; it was a tango tradition in any tango cafe in BA City.

"Look, Rachel, as I had just reciived the news that James Smith and his delagation decided to fly to San Carlos, Barinoche directly after they held a meeting in the U.S. Embassy near Parlermo last afternoon; well, you have to go there as soon as you could; Listen. what you need to do is, to contact Kennedy only and you should not let the other members of the group to notice that..., your ticket is already made, you just go to Aerolinea Argentina's booking office in Cordoba 325 to ask senora Zapata and she will give you directly the ticket and some more information; she is a Chilian clerk but she is working for us." "Should I go now?"

"Yes, better you could go before 5 p.m." Warco said.

"And watch any agent in San Carlos who would bother you, as I know the FBI local agent would work with them together too."

"And we have agent places there too, he will contact you and asistance you also." Warco added.

"Okey, I understand."

"Good luck, Miss Perlsztein." Warco got up saying then left the shop.

It was 4;00 p.m.

"Mozo, la cuenta por favor..." Rachel said to the waiter in distance.

"La cuenta ya esta pagado, senorita." the bartander said.

Rachel got up and ready to leave the bar to go to the travel agency; she noticed through the wooden window, the Museo de tango was not far from there.

It was an old wooden building, a kind of Tango paintings museum, Rachel decided to pay a visit since the time was still a little early.

She walked about 50 meters to get to the gate of the Museo.

The place was a free visiting site. then Rachel stepped on the wooden made short stairs and went slowly in.

There were several floors containing hundreds of old tango paintings, she watched floor by floor; it was quite old house, the higher you got in, the heavier air one could feel; there was nobody in until she arrived the thrid floor and found herself was stopped by two black suit coated guys; they both were wearing dark sunglasses.

Rachel was just standing in the middle way of a channel betweet two walls of paintings.

"No se vaya, senorita..., Vd. tiene que acompananos a arriba." One of the guys said in Sapnish; it was a great suprise for Rachel but she got no choice momantly. She followed them to go to the third floor through a short wooden stairs. Rachel was under two gun points.

"Who are you guys?"

"We are of the SIDE, just don't worry, we won't do anything bad to you; Our boss is expecting you here" one of the agent said, he managed to speak a heavy accent English.

They arrived to a side office located at the rear side of the wooden museum; the air was rather heavy and she was led to meet a middle aged man in his middle fourities who was sitting by a long conference like table; one of the agents invited Rachel to sit on the chair which was just face to the so called boss.

"Please sit down, Miss Perlsztein; my name is Ricardo Marcelo, the district chief of South BA 2, you are standing on my territory." the man said slow and gentle.

"What do you want from me?" Rachel said calmly. "Nothing special and we are not going to bother your liberty neither; but, lady, you have to cooperate with us since we are on the same side; I mean, you government and mine." "I don't understand." Rachel said.

"Yes, you do; And we are watching on you since your first visit to our country; I said that we are on the same side that means we are all against the U.S. government."

"We are not going to bother your mission but to supervise you and in case we will give you any suport." Marcelo added. Rachel said nothing. "Anyway, you are linking with your Embassy here, so we should respect your diplomatic position; on behalf my government, I would like to say sorry for such a bothering; it will not happen again, just trust me; Please remember that whenever you go to anyplace on our territory, we are watching you also protecting you; Now my agent will ride you to the downtown; what I did today is just giving you a message. Now you may go and I am glad to meet you, Miss Perlsztein." Ricardo Marcelo said.

"I wish to go out alone." Rachel said.

"It's your right, lady and thank you again."

"You are welcome." Rachel said in an acid tone. Ricardo Marcelo got up to see her off.

Rachel went back to the street and along the way, she didn't notice anybody was following her. Then she called a cab to go back to her hotel room.

After a cold shower, Rachel called Warco telling him what was happening in La Boca Painting Museum.

"Don't worry about that; it just a routine, you know the SIDE here is having an absolute power they could do what they want even to threst the local President...."

"I asure you, there is nothing for worrying about." Warco added.

"Need I go to Patagonia the same." Rachel asked.

"Sure, lady; the procedure is not changed; I will send somebody to your room the ticket and a VISA card under your present ID name; the person will go to your place at about 9:30 a.m. He is a teen agerr about 18, tall and thin and he will delivery you a UPS package directly to your room; the code is KFC, he will tell you the code, then everything will be ready; I suggest you to go right tomorrow around midday, then you could arrive to Rio Negro the same afternoon or later, don't worry; the Hotel booking confirmation is also included, you just go to live the place, it's a five stars tourism hotel in the downtown." "I wish you luck, Miss Perlsztein." Warco said. "Is James Smith and the guys are already there?" "I suppose so, ot they will arrive a couple of hours later; anyway, our local agent there will contact you as soon as your arriving." Warco added then cut the line off.

Chapter twenty three

San Carlos, Patagonia, April, 2012

When Rachel arrived San Carlos town and settled herself down in the indicative hotel. the local time was around 4 p.m. It was a nice and elegant place with strong German flavor that because the area has long time being occupied by German population after 1945 even a lot of people could handle German language among themself.

Pure green combined light blue lakes, mountains covered white snow on the top; the smalldowntown one could meet old churches, traditional and modern houses, quietness and peaceful like place just setting next to heaven.

Rachel made a simple sightseeing then back to her hotel room; after a cold shower his cellphone vibrated. "Miss Perlsztein, it's me, Warco calling from Buenos Aires; Welcome to San Carlos, the first hand information for you, James Smith and his term had arrived to the place a couple of hours earlier, the group also followed by several U.S. local and Frderal agents for helping the term to make investigations and discovery jobs; You should try to make following-up work with Franky Kennedy also try to get something from Issac Schtok; obviously, he is a MOSSAD agent from Israel, he is partially working with the U.S. government; Listen, FBI agents are also jointing the job; for them the mission is so important politically also scientifically; I suppose you aware what is our goal; One of our local agent there will visit you soon, but you guys need to contact undercoverly; would you understand?"

"Yes, sir, I got it." Rachel said.

"Okey, that's fine and good luck."

The phone line is gone.

Next morning about 9:30 a.m. Rachel down to the hotel dining room on the third floor to take her first breakfast in San Carlos. The pure red brown coated young waiter came to take the order, Rachel peeked the menu and ordered the No.B which was something liked Continental style. The young guy went back to the counter side silently.

After finishing the morning feed, Rachel waved the boy again and ready to pay the cash for the ticket. "Do you know this old mansion young man?" Rachel showed a old faded picture to the waiter after paid the money. The boy took a long look then saying: "Yes, I do, it's now a tourist site but there is no any roadway to get there except to rent a boat or a hydroplane." the boy answered.

"Could the Hotel do the service?" "Sure, lady. We can hire a plane with a pilot for you; just tell me when you wish to pay the visit." "Okey, could you rent a plane with a pilot for me for 2 p.m." "Certainly, madam. It will cost you 90 U.S. dollars for a round trip and you shouldn't stay for over one hour." "Understand, young man. please just do that for me." "Your room number please?" "Room 505." "Okey, lady, I will let you know as soon as the pilot is arriving, first he will ride you to the private airport nearby where you could take it on and back and after that the pilot will send you back to the Hotel. "the boy explained clearly.

"Okey, young man, this is a 100 green note and the rest ten dollars is yours."

"Thank you so much, lady." the boy took the money then left.

The telephone in Rachel's room rang, she answered it immediately. "Miss Perlsztein, the pilot of your reserved plane is waiting here to take you to the water airport." the voive said. "Thank you, I am coming."

Rachel spent a couple of minutes for preparing some necessary staffs putting into her backpack them rushed down to the lobby. She met a very tall handsome guy in his middle thirties, semi- white skinned, thin mustache, he wore a set of sports kind dark gray dress and a pair of leather made high tubeboot.

"Good afternoon, lady. May we go now?" he nodded his head to greet Rachel.

"Sure sir."

"Well, then please follow me, my car is parking outside." Rachel and the guy got on the dark green 1930s antiuque old car, the pilot invited her to sit beside him then speedy the engine heading to the water airport.

"We will take about ten minutes to arrive the water port, actually it's a big lake, you know."

"What's your name?"

"Everybody here calls me Robert."

"Why you are still using this ancient car?"

"Yes, it looks like an old oil can, but I refixed every most modern parts; this waste iron cost a lot of money, you know." The road side view was great along the mountain and trees. Rachel enjoyed the ride and they got arrived the lake side; several hydroplanes in different size were parking on the lake side.

Robert stopped the engine then led Rachel to take a small two seat airplane. Robert invited Rachel to get on the plane first then he opened the door by the other side and went on his driver's seat just next to Rachel.

"Well, lady. Let's just take off and what we need is to cross this lake then passing another mountain hill, the massion is just located not far from the lake side." "It will take about ten minutes only, so enjoy the scene, it's great." Robert said.

"Yes sir." Rachel said.

"May I ask you a question, lady."

"Yes, please..."

"Why did you wish to come here to visit this ancient and old trash house?"

"Because I am reporter of an European historian magazine and we are doing some jobs about some histoical mansion around the world..." Rachel said.

"Hummmm..., it's quite interesting." Robert said.

"Do you travel often to this old house?"

"Not so often, but I knew this house since my childhood." Robert said.

While saying, the plane was just about on landing by the lake side water. "We have not other way to get here?"

"Yes, you may take boat but it needs to pass several short streams and you may take more time." Robert answered.

"Is there any shop or resident around the house?"

"No, lady. It's a very lonely and isolated house."

"Why it got so fameous?"

"I do not really know, people said a very celebrated couple had been staying here for many years but that's just a kind of rumor." Robert said.

Robert got off with Rachel saying, "Lady, you have got one hour time for returning; I am waiting you here; but anyway, watch your ass; Oh..., forgive my expression."

"Why?'

"Nothing, just take care please."

"Thank you, I will."

Rachel began to walk heading to the old house about 100 meters in distance.

It was an huge masion like European style big house just liked an aged classic painting not far from the lake side. It was evdence that even nobody had approached since a very long year; Rachel went in alone step by step, a big living and kitchen combined about over 40 single rooms everything was covered by white cloth but the color turned to be light gray covering a layer of heavy dust; some old paintings still hanging on the wall; Finally, she passed through and arrived the rear gate of the house; there was an abandoned garden accompanying several independant houses; in the deep rear side of the green field one could find more than a dozon graves; she found nothing that could match her investigate matter; then she went back to the front gate along the same road; what happeded was that the hydroplane and the pilot both disappeared from the scene....

It was only 3:20 p.m. but she found herself staying absolutely alone; she even didn't know how to do, it was good bit of scareful around her....... She called her local Polish agent's phone number and after five minutes intending, she got a connection enventfully.

The agent listened her Polish language report then just answered three words back saying:" I will be there right now."

A helicopter arrived about twenty minutes later, a middle aged guy landed the old merchine on the lake side, he waved Rachel just by the plane's gate to call Rachel for boarding on the gray green coated old staff.

Rachel did it quickly and met face to face with the guy; he was a rude but very macho like German and Indian mixed strong man in his late fourties.

"Welcome on board Miss, my name is Carlos." the guy said that then drove the merchine into the low sky.

"Is this old staff belonging to Polish Embassy?"

"No, it's my property but I am one of many Polish souls who are living in this area." Carlos said.

"You know, Carlos, I didn't really study well the mansion while I discovered the pilot had been left...."

"Who presented you that hydroplane?"

"The hotel clerk."

"Don't trust them very much, I suppose the pilot was sent by the local SIDE." Carlos said.

"I didn't suppose they are so much concerning on this case." Rachel said.

"Don't forget we are standing on Argentine terrotory."

"How long have you been living in Patagonia, Carlos?"

"Since my very youth."

"How do you think? I am visiting to the right place?"

"I can say nothing, lady."

While they were talking the helicopter had arrived its base in a green field; Carlos landing the bird carefully until it got difinitely stopped. There was a smallwooden house not far from the base, Carlos led Rachel to go there for a cup of hot coffee.

Rachel's mood was sinking into a deepest downhill; she just realised that she was completely of her own; tricks and betraies were intensively around her.

Carlos offered her to take a ride back to the hotel room, Rachel accepted.

THe next morning after 9:00 p.m. Rachel received a phone call directly from Polish Embassy in BA City; the agent noticed her that James Smith's delegation is on its way to go to San Carlos and what she should do is to contact Frank Kennedy only. Rachel just listened and promised and didn't make any further question; she realized the the situation is in a very complicative state, what she needed to do was to hold herself quietly.

Rachel walked out of the hotel after 10 a.m. ahd intended to relax her mood; she went on walking along the not very wide main street and by chance she met a roadsaide house with a sign on its wall written'Instuto Historical de Patagonia" that called her attention, then she decided to pay a sudden visit.

As soon as she pushed the door in, the first thing she met was a not big living and an empty desk by the rear side wall, several maps and painted pictures were hanging on the wall.

A very thin gentleman in his middle fourties showed up after a couple of minutes, he wore a cotton made dark blue nice quality shirt and confortable light yellow pants.

"Good morning, senorita..." he greeted Rachel with a gentle smile.

"Good morning sir, I just passing here and was attracted by your house, so I dropped in I am reporter from an European gerography magazine and I am here to study the regional culture and local life; My name is Rita." Rachel presented herself.

"Welcome to Patagonia, Miss Rita. My name is Nicola Ponsso, the director of this Institute." Nicola could speak good enough English but carrying a strong south Argentine accent.

"Please sit down, lady." Nicola showed a chiar by the wall and he pulled another chair to sit himself down too.

"Miss Rita, I suppose you are interesting in our regional culture, if there is anything I can do for you?"

"Oh, yes. What I need is something that is still concerning the post war history around this area, especially in Patagonia." Rachel said.

"Well, anything I could know about Patagonis I could tell you."

"Do you have any knowledge about this couple?" Rachel showed the faded picture to Nicola.

Nicola took the picture and looked it for a long while then saying: "I would not give you my real comment, it's been a very long time; it's no more important they were here or not? Yes..."

"Ummm..., I understand that." Rachel said.

"Sorry, do you know this person on the picture?" Rachel showed Nicola Hagen Deutch's picture?"

"Yes, I do but not personaly, he has been here for a long time, it was a fact."

"Was he the treasure manager of the couple?"

"I can't say that, but he was the treasure manager for the Nazis group in Patagonia, it was also a fact."

"All I am saying to you is according to our research result." he added.

"Have you been visited the fameous mansion in San Carlos?"

"Yes, I did once or twice, it's just a ruin representing the past, it's no more important for nothing." Nicola said.

"Could you speak German sir?"

"Sure, I could.'

"But your last name sounds as Italian?"

"Yes, you are right, but my Mom was of German race."

"A lot of population here could handle German language since they are sons or grandsons of German." Posso said.

"There are rumors floating for a long time in Europe saying that Patagonis still is hiding a great treasure of Nazis also including a lot of advanced secret scientic paper also advanced technological know how?" Rachel asked.

"Senorita, I don't believe in that; as you know we are only a culture researching body." Nicola said peacefully.

"But, anyway, I can recommend you to visit an Indian chief whose name is Atapu Tapia, he could speak both his native also Spanish language; if you are interesting in the theme, you could go to visit him; his reservation site is not far from here, I can give you my card and he will receive you as soon as he notice my name, you know, he is one of my best friends, he is

a very wise man but you have got to respect their customs."
Nicola said.

"How could I reach his place?"

"Just rent a cab."

Nicola drew a card from his pocket and written somthing
on the back side then handle to Rachel.

Rachel thanked him then left the place.

She took a simple snack in a food shop cross to the main
street and after a cup of coffee at the end of the meal, she decide
to go to visit the saying Indian chief directly.

She paid the bill and stopped a cab in front the shop, the
driver peeked on the address on the card then speedy the cab
heading to the destination.

Rachel arrived the chief Atapu Tapia's place after about
30 minutes runing, it was a hidden village by the mountain
foot; Indian traditional houses even tent kind of houses were
gathering in that not small area. The first person Rachel met
was an Indian teenager boy around 18, he could speak perfect
Spanish then Rachel asked him to lead her to see the chief
Tapia; the boy was wearing a set of south Indian dress, he was
very strong and well sun tanned; after a couple of minutes
walking, they arrived Tapia's office room, it was straw made
house with both sides windows opened.

Rachel waited outside for a minute until the boy came out
of the room to invite her to go in.

Atapu Tapia was a person out of Rachel's imagination, he
was not so old as she thought; a dark skinned middle aged guy
in his middle fourties; he was wearing a set of faded jeans but
an Indian symbol fur made hat just as Holiwood film showed

Indian chief, he was sitting on a animal fur covered armchair and a long pipe in his hand, he was actually smoking something.

"Welcome, senorita, please sit down." the chief showed Rachel a simple chair by his left hand side.

Rachel also got suprise that the chief could speak quite well Spanish.

"You are speaking a very good Spanish." Rachel said.

"Why not? I am also an Argentine and I was graduate from Universidad de Rio Negro." the chief said with a gentle smile.

"The only thing I could offer you is our Yeba Mate, well, a kind of our native tea if you like."

"Sure, with pleasure.' Rachel said.

"Eduarito......" the chief called the boy's name.

"Ya vengo, jefe.' the boy answered outside the room in distance.

"Yes, my friend Nicola phone me that you need some information around this area?"

"Yes, I do. Mr. Chief.'

"Bueno, just shoot me."

"What I want to know is whether the mysterious couple had been living here?" Rachel showed him the same picture of the couple.

"I can't tell you, senorita. May be yes, may be no. My father knew that better than me but he had been dead for over ten years, you know." the chief said.

"Oh, I am soory. But could you tell me have you ever heard there was a Nazis treasure still hidden in this province?"

"I am not quite sure, may be it was, but honestly I would say, the treasure had been transferd to other place, where? I do not know."

"Are you sure?"

"I can say that, because that is none of my business but one thing I could tell you is that, there is no any Nazis treasure still burying here." the chief dragged a mouthful tobaco from the long pipe. At this moment the same boy came in to serve Rachel Indian tea.

"I understand that, the treasure now is hidding in some other place, is that right?"

"I can tell you neither, but you have to make an account by yourself."

"Could you tell me where could be the new places?"

"Oh..., senorita, it's a hard question. Well, I suggest you to go to the north of the country; well Nazis treasure used to follow Nazis movement; just try to go to the north, who knows, Tucuman, Codoba, Misiones..., everywhere could be."

"What you mean is that Tucuman and Misiones could be the places?"

"I didn't say so, senorita. just try anyplace where has more German population..."

"Excuse me, I have got a little tired." the chief said.

"Thank you so much, chief Tapia, I have already got the sense."

"That's good..."

Rachel left the place and took the same cab back to the city.

After Rachel's leaving, Chief Tapia called the Government House of Rio Negro province and spoke directly to the Governor.

"Senor Governador, soy Tapia, la chica Perlsztein reciem estuve aca y hablo conmigo. Ella esta buscando el tersoro de Nazis."

"Gracias por avisame, senor Jefe Tapia, my voy a prestar attencion por eso."

As soon as Rachel arrived back to her hotel room, a phone call from Polish Embassy in BA City to advise her that James Smith and others had already arrived San Carlos since they didn't success anything in La Falta, Cordoba; the group now is living in Hotel Estrella Sur and the local Polish agent had reserved a room at the same hotel for her; the mission for Rachel was to contact Frankt Kennedy in order to get the first hand information.

After receiving the call, Rachel made a cold shower then decided to check out of the hotel to transfer to Hotel Estrella de Sur.

An hour later Rachel moved into the excellent tourist Hotel with her simple belongings; she checked in a room on the third floor and the Hotel's dinner room and bar were located on the second floor; there were elevators also stairs connecting each floor.

At around 6 p.m. Rachel came down to the dinning salon to have a cup of coffee, as soon as her arriving the first thing she noticed was a group of five or six people were already sitting around a long table about two meters away and evdently James Smith, Dr. Kauffamnn, Issac Schtok, Franky and two more strangers were already sitting there discussing something but none of them paid attention for her presence.

A young waiter coated in dark brown and white uniform neatly neared Rachel for the order. "Buenos tardes, snorita, que desea a tomar?" "Un scrawdriver, por favor." Rachel said with a gentle smile. "En serquita." the waiter dismissed.

Rachel took a chance wrote down some words on a piece of table napkin saying, "Meet me by the lady's room" A couple of minutes later, the same boy came to serve the order, he put the drink softly on the table and ready to leave. "Wait,,," Rachel stopped him saying, "How much is it?" "It's 20 U.S. dollars, madam."

"Okey, here is 30 U.S. dollars, but do me a favor, could you see the gentleman wearing light gray suit, just go to tell him he has a phone call on the counter and give him this paper; would you do that?"

"No problem, miss."

Rachel gave him one twenty and one ten green notes.

The waiter took a chance to go near Franky and telling him there is a phone call for him and pushed the paper slip into his hand too. Franky asked an excuse to go to the counter, James Smith paid a mere attention but didn't say anything.

Franky got up heading to the counter meanwhile he read the paper slip and at this moment, Rachel just passed by for calling his attention, Franky understood immediately.

Rachel just went to the lady's room in the rear part of the salon and standing by the door, Franky came alomost at the same time.

"Dr. Kennedy, my room number is 305, just come to see me, we need to have a talk." Rachel left the message then left the place. Franky got the sense and went back to his seat too. "What was that?" James asked. "Oh, it was a wrong call..." Franky answered. James didn't say anything and went on talking to all the person around.

At about 8 p.m., Rachel's room door was knocked, she was expecting Kennedy's visit; she got up to answer the door and she met Franky standing by the door, then quickly slipped in. "Please sit dow. Dr. Kennedy, this is my room, nothing will be happened." Rachel said.

"I couldn't stay too long, you know we are all under James Smith's order."

"Yes, I am sure it is. What I want to know is that, very simply, did your group find anything important up to now?"

"To tell you the truth, nothing important, by our government seems like to know some details politically more than anything else." Franky said.

"Did they find something from your house in Virginia?"

"Yes, they already hold the most important paper in my other house's garden, therefore, they are following the route to go place after place; if they couldn't find anything here, they would go to Tucuman and Mission..."

"You say Tucuman and Missiones?"

"Yes, that is."

"But I am not interesting nothing of any, you know, what I want is a piece of peaceful life." Franky said.

"What about Issac Schtok?" Rachel asked.

"Well, he is a very smart Jew and he is working for his government too."

"And two other persons who they are?"

"They are two FBI agents, one is from local and the other is of the Federal."

"They paid only attention for looking for some confidential top secrets concerning the national security over this area, even James Smith couldn't know what they are really thinking about..." Franky said. "Okey, Dr. Kenndey, let's make a deal, you just go ahead with them and I will not bother at the moment and whenever your mission will be getting over, I will meet you in the States and then let's talk and work together for our ancient families also for Jewish people..." Rachel said.

"For our families and for Jewish people?"

"Yes, sir."

"What do you mean?"

"I can't tell you know. But thank you Doctor, I have got the information I needed; I will see you soon in the University of Virginia."

"So, you are leaving here, Miss Perlsztein?"

"Not yet. But just take easy; what I need is that you just go on with them and when we will meet again, you should tell me all you have got to know, that's a deal too."

Rachel got up to see Franky off.

The SIDE Argentina had been following up James Smith's group route since the first day they came into Buenos Aires airgate; they tapped any details of their every conference in different Hotel's suite and wired their every conversation onto the record; the Argentine government only wanted to protect her national security also her national property for not being stolen by any foreign government.

Many G countries bought wild south Argentine land and defined them under theri national flags but Argentina would never worry the G countries could sold their territories since they couldn't never be moving her national territory out of

Republic of Argentina'Especially since 2003, Patagonia turned to be a very important area under globle energy and war stradgic points.

James Smith led the U.S. delegation came to south in order to find some evidence that caused a world wide rumer concerning Nazis old treasure and long time hidden most advanced scientic technology including the first German and UFO contact befor 1945 and after 1945. FBI had their Patagonia investigation record after 1945 and followed for many decades but most recently some new evidences pushed the U.S. government to start a new project to clear off the doubtness that related her national security also her regional security.

Argentina never been stopped for being a sleepy tiger and Argentina knew herself better than others G countries. The SIDE agents are watching closely how the U.S. team are moving and what's their real intention; Argentina used to be a cold fox, she never moves beforehand if it would be no need; their intelligence know how was herited by mixing Nazis and Facist system after 1945 or even before.

The U.S. FBI used to be underwavlued the SIDE's capacity.

Rachel moved out from Estralla de Sur the next day in order to avoid James Smith's attention; the NSA agent seemed like feeling something wired from the air around.

Rachel supposed that James Smith would visit the old mansion and its relative area even some places along Los Antes along south Patagonia which goes along the both sides of Chile and Argentina.

After the following couple of days Rachel went on receiving the local Polish agent Pablo Vacakavsky's phone call report saying that James Smith and the team are working hard among the area even moved the U.S. military personels and special instruments and they are looking like to find sometning important especially along Los Antes root side.

Pablo Vacakavsky is an undercoered Polish agent who works as petrochemical engineer in ESSO Sur Patagonia.

Five days later Pablo informed Rachel that two U.S. military helicopters carried two sealed and packed wooden cargos on them and left that seemed like James had got something they wanted.

The second evening Pablo called Rachel saying the U.S. team had left San Carlos and flew away. Rachel made decition to go to Tucuman by plane the next afternoon because she knew that should be James Smith's next spot.

Chapter twenty four

San Miquel de Tucuman May 2012

So called el Jardin de la Republica, San Miquel de Tucuman is a beautiful mountionous town located on the north part of Argentina; its local, native and strong Indian flavor coated thick cultural taste of this ancient city, not big but quite important in the history of the nation. Rachel arrived to the city airport closed to the evening of the next day; she moved in a small downtown hotel, nobody knew her arrival except her electronic connection with Polish Embassy in BA City.

After the evening the downtown of the city of San Miquel converted to be a romantic and quiet place, narrow sidewalk, different type of shops, night bars, food joints, happy people, ancient churches, classic palace style buildings colored the face of this fameous northern Argentine city.

Rachel made a short sightseeing then went back to her hotel room; she was waiting James Smith and his team to arrive most certainly a couple of days later.

A while later she went to the second floor dinning salon to have some light local food, the waiter suggested her to try Embanada Tucumano in fry style with Tucuman made red wine; it was quite delicious after trying them; the so called

Embanada was kind of Italian style snack something looking like Paraguay Chipa, a kind of Indian style snack the same as so called Afaho is also a kind of Argentine popular sanck, a kind of chocolate coated smallround cake jacked with some sweet staff, while she was eating, her cellphone vabrated and the Consul General of Polish Embassy sited in Posada, Misiones called her to give her some indication which was sent by the Ambassador through his mouth saying that she could visit a Polish professor who is now working in the University of Tucuman in San Miquel whose name is Petro Marlinovsky and Rachel could obtain more information she would like to know.; Rachel noted down the contact message and decided to visit the professor the next morning.

She called Marlinovsky next morning, the middle aged voice gentleman invited her to visit his office in the Universidad de Tucuman, faculdad de la historia moderna.

Rachel ariived the place the next morning around 10 a.m., it was a nice sunny day, the beautiful Tucuman sunshine was warm and gentle.

Marlinovsky was a native Polish Argentino in his early fourties who is as tall as six foot two and very slim and thin, he could speak perfect Polish language then they began to converse in their mother idiom.

"Miss Perlsztein, I know your mission is to follow the symbolic route of Nazis treasure which was stolen from Jewish victims who died in Poland during the War II. Tucuman is one of the possible hidden places and it was one of my long years researching items since many decades but I i can see Tucuman would not be the place that Nazis finally hidden their stolen treasure together with many other top secrets and most confidential things; Of course, the couple's death didn't effect nothing about Nazis heritage because they are a crimial gong goes generation after generation; The U.S. team's goal is not on treasure but on others important things, once they would verify that the importance would not go on effect on their current situation then they would withdrow from their researcxhing works; so what you should do is just to watch the U.S. actions and collecting more information, because we have quite diffient goal than theirs. Would you agree mine opinion?"

"Abusolutely, professor." Rachel said.

"Okey, then I could update you something that is only basing on my personal opinion, what you want to find is not in this province."

"Maybe in Misiones?"

"I can say that, maybe, but I also can not say it will be in 100%."' Marlinovsky said.

"So, how is your view?"

"Yes, you should closely follow Franky's way, you just stay on watching, if the U.S. team would go back to the U.S. one day that means their mission will be over and their risk will be also considering over; then you could go back to the U.S. to contact Franky again and his information could help you to just start to realize your operation; but be careful, it might process with great care because MOSSAD would also just begin to start their final mission; as you know, they used to stand on the both sides of the boat, politically and economically."

"Is that your personal view only or some are from our government's indication?" Rachel asked.

"A part of them is my personal view.'

"I see, Professor."

Marlinovsky invited Rachel to eat a simple luch in the compus then Rachel left the school to go back to the hotel room.

Along the route she passed by a road side church that attracted her by its classic and ancient structure although it was not a Jewish Synagague but a Catholic one but Rachel believing in that God is only one, then she stepped in and sitting on one of the empty raw of benches; the interior design of the place was so simple and original that made Rachel feeling confortable and quiet, she maintained her position for several minutes and just wanted to get up and to leave and just found she had a companion sitting beside; its a middle sized guy wearing a traditional Tucuman kind local hat saying in a quite low voice: "Miss Perlsztein, we are watching you along the road, just beware what you are doing...."

Rachel didn't realise such a suprise, she held herself a second then said:" Who are you? what do you want from me?"

"Nothing, Miss Perlsztein, we are of the local SIDE, we are protecting you also watching you, please just behave yourself; you are on our territory, this is Republic of Argentina; please beware of this."

"Good luck." the guy said so then left quickly. It was like a short dream, anyway Rachel didn't feel very good after that.

She walked out of the church and went on for a while then waved a cab to go back to the hotel room.

A couple of days later she received a phone call from BA City saying that James Smith's team went directly to the mountain area around Sam Miquel de Tucuman with special high-tech instrument installed personels working around the targeted points to find something out; the caller was one of the intellgence officer in the Polish Embassy in the Capital City; they suggested Rachel just to watch and waiting for any news to happen.

Rachel more or less had knowledge that the U.S. teams only wish to find something that really related to the U.S. security matter otherwise they would move to Misiones to go on search the final resault; if nothing could be found they would go back to the U.S. and finished the case; that was Rachel's consideration, if it would be so, then she could be sure that Hagen Deutch's case will be removed from the NSA's file.

She informed her Embassy in BA City through phone call that she was going to Posada, Misiones immediately to wait for James Smith's team to arrive to finish their last step's projecty.

She left San Miquel de Tucuamn heading to Posada by renting a Taxi plane with a pilot that took only a couple of hours time to reach the place; she settled herself down in a not big hotel in the smalldowntown Posada which is a border city next to Paraguay. Rachel realized that James Smith's search is basing on a route as Nazis symblo figuer: SWASTIKA; therefore they started from La falta then San Carlos then San Miquel and lasted to Posada but James Smith didn't know the last point; whenever the U.S. team couldn't find the final resault then they would close the case and up to that point, Rachel's plan could just begin to play.

Three days later, James Smith's team arrived and suprisely they came together with three big wooden cargos and they sent them directly to the other side of PIgomayo River. all the three cargos were sealed with the labels written the U.S. Property; these cargos would send to the U.S. Embassy in Asunsion then through there to go back to Washington D.C. because Paraguay is a country completely under the U.S. control.

Polish Embassy in BA City informed Rachel that the U.S. mission could be finished in Misiones but she needed to go on watch what would happen in the following few days.

Rachel and a Polish local agent Jose rent a country house from a famer family close to the river station side in order to watching James Smith's movement; they paid the landlady quite a lot of money.

Near a week passed, finally at the early evening of a sunny day, James Smith's team arrived, a fleet of cars including three big wooden cargos landed on the ferry to cross over the river heading to Paraguay; Rachel and Jose watched from the high position place and filmed the situation they considered that the U.S. teams had finished their mission and would go back to the U.S. directly through Asunsion. What was enclosed in such a cargos were not of Rachel's concern. She decided to go back to Warsovia through Bolivia. She phoned BA City's Embassy before her leaving.

Chapter twenty five

Capital Hill, Washington D.C. June 2012

Senator Jackson Hunt (Republic, Colorado) as the chairman of Intellgnce and dplomatic affairs comettee called a hearing together with the members of the comettee, Senator Cathlline Hess and Sanator Jacob Frankline for undrstanding the details concerning James Smith of NSA and his team's Argentine investigation.

The hearling was taken place under national wide open televised transmission.

Most of media bodies around the area had been presented. Three Santors and their asistants were sitting behind the pannel and on the opposite side, James Smith, Professor Kaufamann and Robert Willians Jr. the international section chief of FBI were all presented.

Senator Jackson Hunt, a tall and handsome young congressman in his early fourties has been heading the comettee for the past two years, he made a short brief then made first Agent James Smith to be the first vitness.

Hunt: Agent Smith, what was your main goal for your last South American trip?

Smith: Under the indirect order of the U.S. Presidency, I did the appointed plan to realize our South American tour that spent about 30 and more days and we found that 80 % of our researching goal had been achieved.

Hunt: Would you tell me what was the real purpose of your project?

Smith: It was something very important concerning our national security matter that couldn't be told to the public or any other body.

Hunt: Including the Snaate of the United State of America?"

Smith: Yes sir."

Hunt; As i know, your team had been traveled around many part of Argentina along Cordoba, Rio Negro, Tucuman and Misiones, is that true.

"Yes sir."

"Did you find anything along the route?"

"Yes sir. We had bought eight wooden cargos back to our land."

"Could you detailed what are those staffs?" Smith: "No, sor."

"Why?"

"Because those staffs are all related to national securitymatters." Smith said. Hunt: "Agent smoth, you didn't answer me any question up to now."

"No sir. I had answered all your questions but something I couldn't tell you without the permission of the President of the United of State of America."

"Why?"

Smith: "You would know the answer up to the year 2045.'

"Agent Smith, you are crossing a little of the limit.'

"No sir, it's the fact."

"We will take ten minutes recess, ladies and gentlemen." Hunt announced. He really didn't know what kind of Q & A they were making?

Senator Catholine Hess went on questioning the FBI agent Robert Williams Jr. after the break.

Hess: Is that true that FBI has been doing investigations of the Couple's whereabouts up to now since the year 1945?" "Yes, madam. I would say we do."

Hess: "Then what's the final result of the finding?" "The finding had been finally ended after 1968." "Then what are you guys still looking about?"

"Something very important to our national security but nothing to do with the War II." "Is that not a relative matter?" "Absolutely not, madam." "What do you mean?" "I can't say that." "Why?" "Because there is a top confidential matter now is holdling by the Degfense Secretary."

"If I insist to know the answer?"

"You have to call the Defense Secretary to be here." "You didn't answer me any question, Agent Williams." "Yes, I did. madam."

The hearling went on for more than 40 minutes but nothing came out; then Senator Jackson Hunt extended the hearing fot the next month.

Warsaw, Poland, June 2012

Rachel went back to Warsaw, the capital City of her homeland, the first thing she did after her arriving was to report to her chief in Agencja Wywiadu (Polish Intellgence

Service) Mr.Jacobo Wananwvczw and they held a 40 minutes long private conference between them; Jacobo told Rachel that a purposed visitng to Isreal would be taken a couple of days later he himeslef and Rachel only and that would be kept as a top secret.

A few days later Wananwvcew took an European flight with Rachel heading to Tal Aviv, Isreal on a midnight plane scheduled to arrive to the City the morning next.

It was a hot June sunny morning, the left the airport and were taken by an offical car belonging to MOSSAD which was coming directly to pick them to its headqueater.

The small black car stopped by a modern building and the agent led them to the fifth floor; it was a long corridor after coming out of the three ways elevators; they follwed several steps after the agent and arriving an office door the copper plant on the door written "SA-005"

The agent pushed the door in and inviting them to go straight in.

An offical in dark blue suit rose up behind his desk ready to welcomeing them with a gentle smile.

"My name is Issac Schtok, the section chief of South American Affairs of our Agency." the guy said. He shook hand with Jacobo and Rachel.

Rachel felt so familiar with this guy, then she said: "Have we met somewhere before?" "Yes, Miss Perlsztein, we had opportunity met in the VU indirectly; thanky you for recognizing me.' Issac Schtok said.

That just called back Rachel's memory. "It's a such a small world." Rachel said.

"Welcome to Tel Aviv again. Miss Perlsztein." Schtok said again.

"It was a pleasure to see you again, Mr. Schtok." Rachel answered.

"Oh, then we are all old friends." Jacobo said.

Issac Schtok invited Rachel and Jacobo into a small inner room where they began to exchange offical opinions over James Smith's South American tour.

"What did they found in Patagoina?" Jacoba asked. "I can't tell you the details since Isreal is also a part of this finding and that will be remainding as a top secret for a long while but I can tell you is the common will between our two nations is just ready to start." Issac said in a very smart way.

"What do you really mean?" Jacoba asked. "Well, what I have said is that James Smith didn't success to find the Nazis treasure; I mean the material value, but they don't care because that's not the real care of the U.S. part."

"So, as you have said, we are just need to begin to start our joint work?" Rachel said.

"Exactly, Miss Perlsztein and what we need is your cooperation mainly."

"Why?"

"Because, Franky's map didn't work, they found nothing basing on the Hagan Deutch's map." Schtopk said. "Is not Franky holding the completely the whole map?" "No, lady. what you are holding in hand is the last part of the completely map and that is exactly what we need your help." Issac said.

"You mean the piece of paper my granddady left?"

"Yes, it is and it's not a only a piece of paper, it's the main part and the last part of the map."

"Is that so important?" Rachel asked by purpose.

"Therefore our two nations need to work together for this time." Issac added.

"For our Jewish people, is that right?" Jacobo said.

"Especially for our Holocaust victims whose generations are still living in everyplace in the world.' Schtok said.

"This is why I bought Miss Perlsztein here." Jacobo added. "Well, Miss Perlsztein, do you need more explanation?" "I suppose not." Rachel said. "Okey, that's fine. As you know James Smith only solved the most important part of the project with his team but that was enough for their national security concern; money is not important for them since the Nazis gold had been melted into Argentine financial system also into world financial rivers since 1945; but most importantly for us is that, as I say. for our Jewish people part, there is still a great piece of treasury mine which is hidding in some place in Argentina and that's why we need Miss Perlsztein's help.

"Why don't you ask Dr. Frank Kennedy to do the job, he is the direct grandson of Hagen Deutch, is that true?" Rachel said.

"That's completely true, madam. but, as you know, your late grandfather Abraham Perlsztein should be the key person for finding out this mysterious treasury." "But Franky is holding almost the completely piece of the map, doesn't he?" "Sure, he has, but that piece of the map now is a piece of trash."

"Why?" Perlsztein asked.

"Because, our term had been traveled and proofed that fact." Issac said.

"You couldn't find anything basing on that map?"

"Absolutely not. Miss Perlsztein, however, according to our information, the only person who could solve that secret is you, madam." Schtok looked deeply into Rachel's eyes saying.

"But, I don't know what are you talking about?"

"If you need any condition, Isreal State is affored to pay you." Issac said smiling.

"I will do my best to find a way but I need to know the plan in order to responding to our government, is that so. Jacobo?"

"Sure, we are both right now repersenting Polish government to concern this case." Jacobo said seriously. "Into our Jewish community, we have nothing couldn't solve." Issac said.

The three persons began to making an innitial plan in Yiddish.

"Why you guys didn't ask Franky to asistant the team to find the treasure?" Rachel asked.

"First of all, Franky is a person who doesn't matter too much money, you know he is a real researching professor, he has got no any bad heritage from his grandfather; of course, he offered his map to the team but that paper didn't help anything; besides, the U.S. government neither paid enough attention for that small matter because they had too much more important things to do." Issac responded Rachel's question.

"Do you think it's a small matter?"

"No, for our Jewish community, it's a great matter both financially and historically."

"But, the U.S. is a G power, it's out of their consideration." Issac added.

"But why the Israel State need my help, they could do it alone, they are also a great power in the Middle East."

"Yes, you are right since you know, the Israel State needs two things together; as the partner of the U.S. and at the meantime to find something for our Jewish community; you know, we are of the world wide Jewish Community, is that true?"

Rachel listened but said nothing.

"Okey, I could do my part as a help but what will be my cut?"

"You are worrying too much. Miss Perlsztein. the Isreal State will award you five million U.S. dollars besides your homeland also will not let you do it in vein, I supposed."

"What will be my role?" Rachel asked. "It's very simple, what we need is your wisdom and your knowledge; I don;t want to say it too clearly, but you know what I mean?"

"Could not Franky do anything? Don't forget he is the granbdson of Hegan Deutch and he is holding the map."

"I had told you that his map is out of any value." "How could you know my knowledge could do any help?"

"Look, if we don't komw it well, today you would not sit here to talk with us." "I am representing MOSSAD Isreal, do you think is not enough serious?" "Okey, let make a plan, but I don't sign any paper." Rachel said.

"We don't need your paper but your brain.' Issac said gently.

"How would be our plan?" Jacobo Wananwvcew asked. "Well, Isreal State will send the most advanced tencnician agents who are speciazied in mountain researching also scientific tasks including three men and two women, they are all as young as Miss Perlsztein and they are also of MASSAD agency; well, Miss Perlsztein must joint our mission and Polish side could also send agents, guards also special technicians to combine the group; we would go to Brasil first and through there we need pass through Iguazu Falls up to Posada, Misiones in order to go back to Argentina for not calling too much attention; well, after entering Argentina, it will be Miss Perlsztein's job to lead us to go the place we need to go, because she is the only person who knows the correct target."

Issac said.

"When we will take the operation?"

"Within five to six days."

"You know, now we are on June, the weather in Argentina would be cold or not?"

"But, the climate is still okey if we go to the north part of the country." Schtok said.

"Why do you know we have to go to the north?"

"Evidently, Franky Kennedy couldn't find anything in any part of the country after a monthful intensive jobs."

"Are you sure that north is the right direction?"

"I don't know, you should ask Miss Perlsztein." Issac saying eith a smart smile.

"Okey, basically, let's do that, so when and where we will meet all together?" Wabawvecw asked.

"How about June 15th in Jerusaleam?" Schtok said.

"Why Jerusaleam?"

"Because we need to pray first at the saint place and the second, our Primer would like to meet every member of the team."

"Okey, it sounds good.'

"Then it's a deal." Issac said.

"Sure, sir. We Jewish never promise for the second time."

"Very good, sir."

Jacobo and Rachel left the office then took a flight the same day back to Poland.

Chapter twenty six

Salta, Argentina June 2012

Isreal and Poland jointed team arrived Salta City, northeast of Argentina on 20th of June after they had traveled through Brasil and entered the small town Ponta Pora and from there they hired a tourist bus to go first to Encarnacion then crossing over Parana River to get the border city of north Argentina, Posada, they went on passing Corrientes, Resistencia and after a long run to arrive Salta City.

The jointed team consisted about twenty members including the both countries scientists, technicians, special agents also two Isreali special armed soldiers; they paid money for every gates they had passed for not calling attention since they knew in South American countries everything could be sloved with money; money could be used as visa or any negociations. They left Jerusaleam on June 15th and spent five long days to get the destination.

The team settled down in Hotel Colonial, a quite modern tourist hotel in downtown Salta city. Isreali special agent of MOSSAD Johan Grossman was appointed as the Capitan of the team; he was a strong built guy in his middle fourties; Miss Perlsztein was considered as main brain for this mission.

Salta is a strong Indian colored city, the whole city representing its colonial time flavor since 17th century and up to now, the city still maintaining over 70% its old face except some new and modern constructions after 1970; Plaza 9 de Julio is the main park in downtown Salta; fameous Calbilto House, Cathedral and many many classic old churches decorating a special tast of this cultural place; the city was quiet and full of green, mountains and simple people; it looks like a place out of heaven.

The members of team first made a city round sightseeing after their arrival then they took one day break in the Hotel in order to discuss and preparing the operation for the saying mission.

Johan Grossman made a general review over the project during the time they gathered in the big tea salon in Yiddish; that took about near 40 minutes, then the group dismissed to enjoy freely around.

Grossman called Perlsztein aside and they sat by a small round table near the window in order to exchang the innitial view.

"Where we are going first? Miss Perlsztein?"

"Well, the first step we have to do is to take the fameous so called Tren en Las Lubes." Rachel said.

"What's that?"

"It's a 210 and something long kilometers hig railway which starts from Salta railway station along the Los Antes hills, the highest level is about 4000 meters above sea level."

"And...?"

"And we need to get off at Estacion Meseda, it is located about 109 kilometers far from Salta station."

"How long we should take?"

"About three hours more or less." Rachel said.

"And after that?"

"After that, it will be my decision. Capitan Grossman."

"You bet." Grossman smiled.

"When are we going?"

"The best time is tomorrow morning around 9 a.m."

"Then we could have lunch there in the midday."

"Exactly, if we could find some place to eat." Rachel said.

The morning next the whole team moved to Salta railway station around 9 a.m. ready to go to take so called Trens en Las Lubes; The station was looking so ancient and traditional as old as 1850, silence, quietness, very few passengers; it looked like a isolated place outside of Argentina.

The Capitan accompanied Rachel to get some information from the booking office; the old Indian like clerk sold them total 24 tickes to go to Estacion Meseta about 109 kilometers away from Salta main station.

All the members got on the train and everyone found a confortable place to enjoying the three hour long exciting trip.

The long snaky train left the station about 9:30 p.m. and scheduled to arrived Meseta near the same midday.

Capitan Grossman sat shoulder by shoulder with Rachel chatting in Yiddish; the team was looking like a group of foreign tourist. The route scene along the way was great. the passengers were traveling above thousands meters above the sea level; actually they were passing through clouds around and different colors of mountains far and near, reddish and bluish, green ones and dark gray ones, quietness and peaceful like feeling made them just staying out of the real world. there were very few persons whenever the trans stopped by every station, something liked an empty country; the sneky trans went on and on.....

After three hours and something more the team arrived the indicated station: Estacion Meseta, just 109 kilometers far from the Salta Main Station.

It was a very silence and isolated place, Capitan Grossman led the whole team got off of the train; only a cou[ple of Indian blooded like empolyees were caring the station.

Rachel neared one of them to get some information to see where the team could get a place to stay.

"Salir de la estacion y Vds pueden ver una casa grante viejo y alla Vds pueden pasar la noche, hay comidas tambien." The eldely clerk told Rachel in Spanish.

"Gracias senor. Vd es muy amable." Rachel turned to Grossamn and said so and so in Polish.

The team left the old station heading to the place was called as an Inn to rest their bodies.

There was a woonden sign written in black paint "La Casa de los Amigos"; it was a huge and long house with about half dozon rooms, kitchen, shower also a small bar where could serve coffee and Coca Cola and something else.

They checked in the "Hotel" and an old Indian guy served them with a smile. The twenty four persons of the team occupied the total six rooms of the hotel; not very confortable but they were settled. That day was very hot since it was in South America winter, the temperature in north Argentina reached 37 degree C while Buenos Aires was only at 17 degree that day and the south Argentina was in heavy snow. They got the weather report through the old man's radio. The Hotel had not fans neither, but luclily they got a small water pool around, the water was in green color, very very clean; they were in Salta, a very beautiful and natural clean place.

Rachel and Grossman planed the first task for the second day, what they needed was to travel 27 kilometers south from Meseta.

Grossamn gathered all the members to explain the plan and they would need to camp at the place after they would arrive the destination. Rachel told the old man what they wanted was a truck with a guide; the old guy said he owned an old truck that could be served but he needed some bucks; Rachel gave him fifty pesos, they guy was satified. He promised Rachel that the truck and guide would be ready the morning next.

About 9 a.m. the next day, an very old truck was prepared for the team; the old man brought a young Indian native guy who would be the driver also for serving as the guide.

All the team got on the truck liked soldiers, Rachel sat besiade the driver Jose; Rachel told Jose in Spanish what they wated was to go a place about 27 kilometers to the south and find a place whare was having a cross on the hill.

Jose nodded that seemed like he knew more or less the existence of such a place.

The mountain route was narrow and risky, but for a local Indian was not a hard job; he drove quiet and steady and after about one hour slow run, the truck arrived a place by the moubtain root..

Jose stopped the car engine.

"Donde estamos?" Rachel asked.

"Aca es el lucar Vds deben qure llegar." Jose said in Spanish.

"Oh, esta muy bien, Raher pushed twenty Pesos into Jose's hand.

The native guy was in his heaven.

"Cucharme, Jose. nosotros necesitamos quetar aca para vario horas y depues Vd. tiene que llevanos a la vuelta, esta bien y yo me voy dar vente Pesos mas para el vieje, esta bien?"

"Esta muy bien, senorita, Vd no se fijar, vayase con tranquilo, me voy espera aca hasta Vds terminar el trabajo." Jose said honestly.

"Muy bien, joven." Rachel said.

Rachel said to Grossman so and so and the Capitan smiled.

"Let's go guys, this is the place and let's begin to work. "Grossman led everyone to start to climb up to the hill.

"What we need to find is a place where we could find a cross." Rachel said. "What do you mean?" Grossman asked.

"In Spanish means Santa Cruss de la sierra, that means a Christian cross on a small mountain."

"Oh, okey, I got it." Grossman said.

The whole team began to clim up to the hill slowly, the north Argentine winter sun was warm but dry; the mountain trail was narrow and quite still but those guys were all trained in special skill that didn't bother them too much.

After near half an hour they reached the first wave of the hill and found a very old abandoned Christian church was standing there; it looked like more than hundred years old at least and a green field was not far away from the church and through that direction they could see another small hill in not very far distance. Grossman took out his telescope began to watch around and after a couple of minutes he said: "That it is."

"What is it?" Rachel asked.

"As you said, Santa Crus de la sierra..."

"Really...?"

"Sure, lady." Grossman said smiling and passes the instrument to Rachel.

"Oh.. my God, there it is." Rachel watched and confirmed.

"Ladies and gents, let's go for that place, only 500 meters more." Grossman said to the team.

Fifteen minutes later all the members were arrived the target place one after the other.

There was a wild and old cementary extended around the low hill and an old wooden cross was standing on the top of the hill.

"Let's first to eat our dry lunch and drinks and after that, let's work." Grossman decleared the order.

"How do we begin? Miss Perlsztein." Grossman asked.

"I don't know, anyway, first let's take a look from the cementary field."

"You mean, through the tombs?"

"Exactly." Rachel answered.

"Do you know what we are looking for...?"

"Absolutely."

"We are finding a huge treasury, it couldn't be under the sun." Rachel added.

"Under the hill or under the deads?"

"Let's just see, Capitan, we have got such a professional team."

Rachel began to drink her water bottle just took out of her backpack.

The midday sun got harder.

"First let's work on the hill today to see what will be happened this afternoon..."

Grossman said to himself.

Rachel said nothing.

The team first standed up their tants around the working site and preparing to start the task after 2 p.m.

The Indian guide Jose was waiting for the downhill truck drinking mate and eating local dampling Chipa.

Around 2 p.m. Gross, an ordered the team to begin to search on the smallmountain hill. They used different kinds of instruments to scanning the soil under; the north Argentine earth has the same dark reddish color as Paraguay and Brasil besides the soil was not tight; the total 24 persons working extending over the small hill for more than two hours and found nothing; they withdrew back to their tants for a break and discussion; the ending opinion was that the hill was hidding nothing underneath.

"Let's begin on the cementary tomorrow morning." Rachel suggested.

"On the cementary, are you crazy?" Grossman said.

"Maybe I am crazy, but it will be the only possibility, otherwise there is nothing here."

"Okey, just as you say, it's something related to your grandfather, so you are the owner.' Grossman joked.

"it's nothing to do with my granddady; it's something to do with Jewish race."

The whole team went back to the 'Hotel' by Jose's truck without any success.

Rachel went to talk with the owner of the place for preparing some asado and wine as dinner for all the team; Rachel gave the old guy 100 pesos for covering the cost, the old man said it was not enough but for expressing Salteno's friendship he would like to put the rest cost for welcoming foreign friends. Rachel thaked him since she knew it was a lie.

The old big house converted a happy restaurant after 8 p.m. The Argentine province people used to make a great asado and almost every province in Argentina could produce very good vino tinto.

After the food the owner and his wife also some Indian workers danced their traditional show to entertain the guests.

They slept with hotness and mos1quitos but they were all very tired.

The norning next, the owner made cafe con leche and some Indian kind of sanwitches as breakfast; everybody ate it.

After 9 a.m. the team went back to the same site for the second try.

There were hundreds of old tombs extending over the field.

Several technicians used their metal dectors separately looking for in different part of the cementary. Most of the tombs were of Christian ones; most of them were aged except some were made after 1945 according the death date marked on the stones.

Rachel walked along the rows of the tombs, one next one, there were so many some with pictures, some only marked a cross on the stone. Moss and straw everywhere.

She was walking on and back along the tombs and trying to search something special through her dark green sunglasses under the strong sunshine.

One naked tomb called her attention because the surface of the tomb only written the year 1946 to 1962 on the middle lower part of the tomb, the grave was neighbored with several almost the same age graves. Rachel took several picture through her iPad; she didn't say anything.

After 5 p.m. Grossman decided to finish the daily work and ordered to go back to the boarding place.

The night was bored enough, most of the mombers were listening radios or musics or chating; the owner of the house was busying to serve some drinks or mate tea.

Rachel sat on a chair trying to check the picture she made during the same afternoon's search; she enlarged the tomb picture in different sizes trying to find some clue; a line of pale yellow line called her attention that seemed like a line of faded letters but she couldn't read it clear with the most higher degree's marcoscope. She decided to check it out the next day.

She showed that for Glossman and some other technicians, they rose the same interests and attention too. The team returned the site again the third day morning.

The first thing they started to do was to check the saying tomb stone and after near one hour studying, most of the specialist said that the line of the letters seemed written as:

D x xxx Deuxxh

"THe second word is Deutch." Rachel said.

"Do you mean this Deutch has something to do with Hagan Deutch?" Grossman asked.

"Yes sir.'

"But the first word doesn't start with H."

"Let's see. Capitan." Rachel said with a smart smile.

The same night Rachel and Grossman discussed the result of the day's work; The Capitan wanted to know why Rachel paid such a attention for the saying tomb. "It's still a secret, I won't tell you but the important thing is that tomorrow we need to make test on the tomb and the area around." Rachel said.

"So it's a top secret?"

"Almost.'

"Well, I understand." Grossman nodded.

The next morning, Grossman only led two technicians and Rachel to go back to the site and made a test; the signal showed postive resault.

"Let's go back home and we have got to discuss." Grossman said. The team gathered the same night and decided to go back to their cooresponded home countries immediately to wait for a further order.

"Do you know why we need to go back right now?"

"Of course I know, first because we had reached the first step target and the second, because SIDE Argentina had began to follow us; we need to leave as soon as possible." Rachel said. The team traveled back through the same way and bought tickets to go back home through Bolivia. It was near the end of June.

Chapter twenty seven

Tel Aviv, Isreal July 2012

Rachel and Grossman traveled again to Isreal after a short while of returning to their homeland; they met Issac Schtok in his MOSSAD's office again; they made an hour long meeting.

"Okey, since now the case will under MOSSAD's hand and you guys just waiting for our good news in Poland." Issac said.

"I suppose this time your are going to bring the treasure back and not to hunt Erchman after the War." Grossman joked. "Don't worry, we MOSSAD guys used to do very clean and rapid jobs." Issac said. "So, how long do you suppose the mission could be done?" "We will first ask our Primer Minister's permission then our operation will start immediately; don't worry, everything has been under a perfect planning for a not short time and as soon as we would finish the operation then our two nations should make an open communication to the Jewish people worldwide." Issac said.

"How much value you should estimate for such a fortune?" Grossman asked. "Well, as you know, most of the Nazis gold had been melting into Argentine and world financial streams after the 1945 but the treasure that confined by Hagen Deutch and his group we could not give a correct figuer but several tons of jewelry, diamond, precious stones, gold and others valuable stones should be over three to five trillions U.S. dollars in today's value; besides tons of foreign currency which were published before the War II could be turned to be modern currency through world G-countries that counts a lot of money; well those great value are belonging to world Jewish communities and the government of Isreal State will secure it to return to Jewish community; no penny will be lost." Schtok decleared the policy of the decision of the State of Isreal. "I am satisfied the policy and I trust it will be done very soon." Grossman said.

Grossman and Schtok signed a joint communication after the meeting. Rachel and Grossman flew back to Poland a couple of hours after they left Issac's office.

Mossad's missionary group total 15 special agents left Isreal heading to Argentina through a special route.

They needed 15 days to complete their mission and the Embassy of Isreal in Buenos Aires was under the order to supervise the process of the saying operation.

The missionary group took Paraguay as the transfer country to go into Argentine territory secretly and they had to avoid Argentine SIDE's eyes too. They motivated the local Jewish agents who were siting in the north part of Argentina also theri private planes, trucks to joint the operation. The undercovered digging works took almost ten nights, six big sized old cooper made containers found under the deep earth; the agents worked hard to move them down to the foot of the hill then they paid a great amount of money to buy local Indian workers to transfer them back to Salta City through the train;

In order to pass Paraguay and Argentine border they needed to buy the corrupted both sides Migeration officers and Military control gates with a lot of green bills; South American people love U.S. dollars more than gold; while money talks, moneys dance.

As soon as the cargos passed into Paraguay territory, then there was no more problem because the transportation trucks ran directly to the Isreal Embassy in Asunsion and from there the cargos flew back to Isreal via diplomatic flight; In Paraguay, any country could be a great power and do what she wants.

On 30 of July, the government of Isreal State officially announced the great news to the Jewish organizations worldwide.

The U.S. State Department didn't make any comment.

Miss Rachel Perlsztein was called by the President of Poland and awarded her a paycheck in five million U.S. dollars to answer her great effect for the mission. After the ceremony, Grossman neared Rachel and congraturated her. "How did you idenfied that tomb as Hagen Deutch's treasury hidden place?" "Because I recognized his real first name." Rachel said simply. "I remember the innitial letter of the first word was D, is that right?"

"Yes, it was."

"Do you really want to know?" Rachel said.

"Yes, I do. if isn't still a secret."

"Of course not."

"THe letter D means David." Rachel said.

"What happened that David had anything to do with Hagen Deutch?"

"Because David was hagen Deutch's real Jewish first name."

"Was that a secret indicated by your grandfather?'

"No sir. I spent my great strength to get it through my personal investigations." Rachel said.

"As I know, you heritaged your grandfather's the last piece of the map of the treasure?"

"Yes, I had, but now the map is no more useful."

"How did your grandfather got the last part of the map?"

"I really don't know, it was a secret between he and Hagen Deutch, they both had passed away for a long time."

"Very good. Miss Perlsztein, are you going to take a long vocation?" "I don't know, maybe I would go to the UV to visit professor Franky Kennedy." Rachel said. "So long, Miss Perlsztein, I wish you lucky." "Thank you sir."

Rachel Perlsztein went back to her hotel room and planed to go back to her hometown once where her mom was buried and after that she would plan a U.S. trip.

Chapter twenty eight

University of Virginia, September 2012

Dr. Frank Kennedy was sitting behind his office desk, the lady secretary slipped in to inform him that a young lady is here to visiting him, her name is Rachel Perlsztein. It was a sunny Wednesday 2 p.m.

"Please just let her in." Franky got up from his confortable chair ready to meet the Polish young lady again. Rachel appeared in a pale blue lady's suit, light blue sunglasses, light and gentle lady's make-up. "Miss Perlsztein, it's so nice to see you again." Franky was suprised of the Ploish lady's visit. "Such a long time, Dr. Kennedy; I am here in the U.S. again; how have you been in your South America trip anyway?"

"It was a great historical and tourism experience since I went there for an official mission." Franky said. "Did you fullfilled your official mission?" "Thanks to God, everything we needed to find was made and the government was very satisfied for our effects." "What you guys really found? May I know?" "What we have found were classified as top confidential national security; so I have to seal them for the rest of my life, you know." Franky answered.

"Oh, I understand, may be we would know in the future."

"Yes, maybe up to the year 2050."

"Are you kidding me?"

"It's true, lady." Franky said seriously.

"I overheard that you are appointed as the new U.S. Ambassdor to Argentina, is that true?" Rachel asked.

"Yes, it's true."

"Do you like the job?"

"I don't know, but to return to my grandfather's ancient past will be a kind of mysterious attraction."

"Do you know your grandfather was a Jew?"

"Yes, now I know." Franky said lightly.

"And you also learnt that he was a great Nazis criminal?"

"Yes, I did. lady."

"Well, anyway, your ancient past was nothing to do with you; you are a pretty good historian." Rachel smiled gently.

"Thank you, lady. you are bery kind."

"Dr. Kennedy, if you don't mind, would you tell me did you practiced the map you had in your hand?"

"No, lady. it was a piece of waste paper after FBI verified it; because the last part of the map has been lost for a long time." Franky said.

"Besides, the U.S. Government was not interested in such a thing; they paid attention for several most important cases." "But, did they returned that map to you?" "No, they told me the map has been destroyed." Franky said. "Do you know where was the lost part of the map?" Rachel asked.

"I suppose I do know but it's no more important to me.'

"Ummm..., you are a honest gentleman."

"Thank you.'

"Dr. Kennedy, as a historian who majoying in researching the post war modern history, do you know how was your grandfather's Jewish first name?"

"People called him as Davil, Evil and somthing very similiar in pronunciation..." Franky said.

"You are a smart person, Professor."

"Do you know my grandfather's real Jewish first name, I mean the given name?"

"Yes, I do."

"How did you know that?"

"I can't tell you, but now it's useless anymore for the case."

"Are you going to publish any professional book about the case Professor?"

"Maybe, yes, but first I have to live in Argentine for a period of time and than I would decide to write it since you know Argentina is a very interesting Facist and Nazis based country and it still is." Franky said.

"I agree."

"Would you visit there? Miss Perlsztein? As I know, your grandfather had also spent quite a lot of time in that country along his lifetime."

"Yes, he spent a long time with your grandfather, first they were a couple of great lovers and afterwards, two great enemies." Rachel said.

"Well, the old time had gone."

"Yes, Doctor. We have nothing to do with Nazis, we are of the young generations."

"Yes, now I know we are all Jews."

"Maybe the Nazis did crimes, but we Jews also did great crimes."

"I have got the same opinion, lady."

"Will you write any book concerning your South American trip, Miss Perlsztein?"

"Yes, maybe, but in English because I would like the whole world to know the story." Rachel said..

"Could you update me the title of the book?"

"The book will be titled as DAVID'S CODE because you will also be presented in the book." Rachel smiled secretly.

"Um..., David's Code; it's a very good title and you are a very smart lady too."

"Thank you.'

"Miss Perlsztein, may I invite you for dinner tonight?"

"Okey, I accept it for our both grandfathers sake."

"How long you will be staying in here?"

"Well, maybe for a couple of weeks or less.."

"And when are you going to take the office in Buenos Aires, Dr. Kennedy?"

"Very soon, before the fifth of October." Franky said.

"That's good, maybe I will visit you there before the Christmas." Rachel said.

The End

Also by Jings Chen

The Boss

Chicago Time

About the Author

==

Jings Chen spent near 30 years in Argentina and experienced most bloody and turbulence time since 1977 up to 2003; his life fate allowed him to contact high level political, military also intelligence fields along the years but that also let he and his beloved late wife lost everything they got including their just born son to remain missing since September 1983; David's Code could let you to visit many beautiful places of that natural rich and attractive country, Latin romantics and strong passion and deep cowboy feelings...; This book is no need any celebrities writers to make commercail endosements neither needs New York Times to list it on its weekly paper slip because, the book itself is of a great Latin American imagination no one could invent the same without knowing the true flavor of such a wonderful land; don't hate Argentina, because she herself is alwaysinnocent.... He is living in Taipei and David's Code is his third book after The Boss and Chicago Time

==

Acknowledgements

The person who achieved me for being a writer was my late wife Raquel Czertok de Chen, a Cambridge taught English language teacher and she corrected all my any English writing materials along our several decades lives living together without her love and hearty and gentle accompanying through such a long years, hardness or happiness, sweetness or sadness...; I would never ever forget her; and I suppose after my works had been published one after the other; her soul might smile with warm tears looking on me from the sky....

My great appreciation goes to Mr. John Edward of Partridge Publishing Singapore, He is the person who encouraged me and guided me into this beautiful filed and with his patience and hearty assistance also a long term friendly consultation that allowed me to realize my dreams come true one after the other, I would never forget his gentlemanship and friendship forever.

The same feeling I would like to pay to Miss Shelly Edmunds who is my publishing consultant as well and her ladyship and hearty assistance helped me to achieve the first two books' cover also interior design; besides she was born in the same year as my missing son; therefore her deep feeling and sympathy effected my heart that value very much along my headest monent caused my wife's passing away in 2009; my first book The Boss was born on January 2014 first through former Trafford Publishing Singapore, today's Partidge Publishing Singapore; Shelly also did my second book Chicago Time's design on April 2014.

My specail thanks also need to pay to Miss Nancy Acevedo, my website designer who is a very gentle and kind young lady as Shelly.

Mr. Chris Lodovice of Author's Learning Center who is a perfect young gentleman also now one of my firends related to the publishing house; I had learnt many things through his direction.

Miss Janine Perez, Miss Emily Laurel, Miss Jacqueline Yu, Miss Vanessa Marzo those young ladies all did my gentle help also hearty kindness; I won't forget them along my writing way since now on.

Mr. Hans Panares suggested me a lot of marketing knowledge and I also learnt much from him, although I didn't make any business with him but he is a good guy and I appreciate him also very much.

Miss Kelly Smith, she appeared to assistant me to do marketking job for my first book, although she has strong character and paid me less attention but I suppose she is also a nice lady.

My specail thanks to Miss Aira Teologo who called me six months earlier before my fist book to innitial my root idea but she had left Trafford office and later John Edward followed her step to realize the birth of my first small book; I remember her as a very nice and professional young lady. Also Mr. John Perez who had once phone talk with me.

In one word, without Partridge Publishing team I would still stay in my empty dreams.

Thank you everyone and thanks to God who brought me into Partridge Publishing, a direct branch part of Penguin Random House Company.